"Sit down," Clint said. "We still have some talking to do."

Westin sat back down.

"About what?"

"I think it's time you answered the main questions for me."

"And what are they?"

"What's going on?" Clint asked. "That's one."

"And the other?"

"Who's heading up this group of men that killed Bags and the other five?" Clint asked. "Who's got it in for your boss that he needs gun help?"

"Uh, I think that's for Mr. Powell to tell you."

"Well, I didn't ask him," Clint said. "I asked you."

DON'T MISS THESE
ALL-ACTION WESTERN SERIES
FROM THE BERKLEY PUBLISHING GROUP

THE GUNSMITH by J. R. Roberts
Clint Adams was a legend among lawmen, outlaws, and ladies. They called him . . . the Gunsmith.

LONGARM by Tabor Evans
The popular long-running series about Deputy U.S. Marshal Custis Long—his life, his loves, his fight for justice.

SLOCUM by Jake Logan
Today's longest-running action Western. John Slocum rides a deadly trail of hot blood and cold steel.

BUSHWHACKERS by B. J. Lanagan
An action-packed series by the creators of Longarm! The rousing adventures of the most brutal gang of cutthroats ever assembled—Quantrill's Raiders.

DIAMONDBACK by Guy Brewer
Dex Yancey is Diamondback, a Southern gentleman turned con man when his brother cheats him out of the family fortune. Ladies love him. Gamblers hate him. But nobody pulls one over on Dex . . .

WILDGUN by Jack Hanson
The blazing adventures of mountain man Will Barlow—from the creators of Longarm!

TEXAS TRACKER by Tom Calhoun
J.T. Law: the most relentless—and dangerous—manhunter in all Texas. Where sheriffs and posses fail, he's the best man to bring in the most vicious outlaws—for a price.

THE Gunsmith

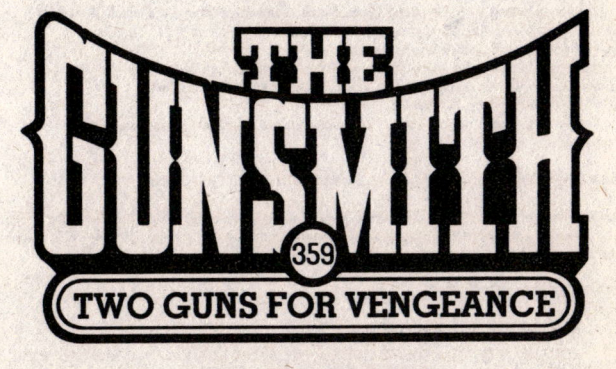

359
TWO GUNS FOR VENGEANCE

J. R. ROBERTS

JOVE BOOKS, NEW YORK

THE BERKLEY PUBLISHING GROUP
Published by the Penguin Group
Penguin Group (USA) Inc.
375 Hudson Street, New York, New York 10014, USA
Penguin Group (Canada), 90 Eglinton Avenue East, Suite 700, Toronto, Ontario M4P 2Y3, Canada
(a division of Pearson Penguin Canada Inc.)
Penguin Books Ltd., 80 Strand, London WC2R 0RL, England
Penguin Group Ireland, 25 St. Stephen's Green, Dublin 2, Ireland (a division of Penguin Books Ltd.)
Penguin Group (Australia), 250 Camberwell Road, Camberwell, Victoria 3124, Australia
(a division of Pearson Australia Group Pty. Ltd.)
Penguin Books India Pvt. Ltd., 11 Community Centre, Panchsheel Park, New Delhi—110 017, India
Penguin Group (NZ), 67 Apollo Drive, Rosedale, Auckland 0632, New Zealand
(a division of Pearson New Zealand Ltd.)
Penguin Books (South Africa) (Pty.) Ltd., 24 Sturdee Avenue, Rosebank, Johannesburg 2196,
South Africa

Penguin Books Ltd., Registered Offices: 80 Strand, London WC2R 0RL, England

This is a work of fiction. Names, characters, places, and incidents either are the product of the author's imagination or are used fictitiously, and any resemblance to actual persons, living or dead, business establishments, events, or locales is entirely coincidental

TWO GUNS FOR VENGEANCE

A Jove Book / published by arrangement with the author

PRINTING HISTORY
Jove edition / November 2011

Copyright © 2011 by Robert J. Randisi.
Cover illustration by Sergio Giovine.

All rights reserved.
No part of this book may be reproduced, scanned, or distributed in any printed or electronic form without permission. Please do not participate in or encourage piracy of copyrighted materials in violation of the author's rights. Purchase only authorized editions.
For information, address: The Berkley Publishing Group,
a division of Penguin Group (USA) Inc.,
375 Hudson Street, New York, New York 10014.

ISBN: 978-0-515-15012-4

JOVE®
Jove Books are published by The Berkley Publishing Group,
a division of Penguin Group (USA) Inc.,
375 Hudson Street, New York, New York 10014.
JOVE® is a registered trademark of Penguin Group (USA) Inc.
The "J" design is a trademark of Penguin Group (USA) Inc.

PRINTED IN THE UNITED STATES OF AMERICA

10 9 8 7 6 5 4 3 2

If you purchased this book without a cover, you should be aware that this book is stolen property. It was reported as "unsold and destroyed" to the publisher, and neither the author nor the publisher has received any payment for this "stripped book."

ONE

Andrew Powell sat at his desk, waiting.

He lived in a two-story Southern-style mansion, complete with white columns. This was not the South, though. The house was situated twenty miles outside of Phoenix, Arizona. In fact, it was closer to the small town of Brigham.

Powell was a wealthy man who had always thought that money could buy anything. Love, respect, power. All of it. And for a long time, it had. It was only lately that some of it had begun to fade away.

A woman entered the room tentatively. She was tall, slender, still lovely at fifty, ten years younger than her husband of twenty years.

"You're brooding," she said.

"Yes."

"And you still don't want to tell me why?"

"Andrea—"

"I know, I know," she said. "This is your business, and you don't want me to be involved in your business."

"That's right."

"Do you want some coffee?"

"No, thank you."

"A drink?" she asked.

He picked up his half-filled goblet of wine and showed it to her.

"Very well, then," she said. "I'll be off to bed. Will you be coming?"

"Soon," he said. "Very soon."

As she turned to leave the room, he looked at the grandfather clock against the wall. It was almost 9 p.m. He'd expected to have some results before this.

He sipped his wine.

Andrea Powell was walking across the entry foyer toward the stairway when the front doors slammed open. She cried out in surprise and fear as men poured in through the doorway.

She turned to face the intruders. Some of them had other men slung over their shoulders. Others had guns in their hands.

They spread out in the foyer. Another man entered, walked directly up to her, and asked, "Where is Andrew Powell?"

"What do you want with my husband?" she asked.

"I've brought back something that belongs to him," the man said.

"And what's that?"

The man smiled and gestured with one arm, encompassing the men behind him.

"These men."

"All these men?" she asked, not understanding.

"No," the man said. "Not all of them." He leaned toward her to give his words extra weight. She shrank from him.

"Just the dead ones."

TWO GUNS FOR VENGEANCE

* * *

Andrew Powell heard the ruckus in the hall, sat up at his desk, but did not move.

"Andrea?" he called. "What was that?"

There was no answer, but he did hear voices. Rather than going to see what was happening, he opened a desk drawer and took out a gun.

"Your husband?" the man asked.

"Who are you?" Andrea asked instead.

The man studied her. He was tall, well built, in his forties, with steel gray eyes that bored into her.

"My name is Ben Randolph. You're very beautiful," he said. "And you have sand. What are you doing with a man like Powell?"

"I—we're married."

"I know that," he said. "That wasn't what I was questioning."

She stared at him, not sure what to say.

"Your husband?"

"This way," she said. "I'll take you to him."

Powell kept his eyes on the doorway to his office, held the gun in his lap. When Andrea appeared, he heaved a sigh of relief, but before the sigh was complete, he saw Randolph right behind her.

They entered the office, followed by other men.

"Mr. Powell," Randolph said. "We've come back to return something of yours. Gentlemen?"

He stepped aside, and Andrea followed his lead. Five of his men, all carrying dead men over their shoulders, moved forward. They each dumped a dead man in front of Powell's desk.

"Next time you hire some gunmen to kill me," Randolph said, "find a better class of men."

Powell stared at Randolph. He couldn't see the dead men who were piled on the floor because they were hidden by his desk.

"You want to use that gun you're holding in your lap, Andrew? Come on, show some gumption. Take a shot at me."

Powell found the gun in his lap growing heavier and heavier.

Randolph walked up to the desk and put his hand out. Slowly, Andrew Powell lifted the gun and handed it to Powell.

"Attaboy," Randolph said. "So the situation hasn't changed, Andrew. The same deadline is still in force."

Randolph turned and waved to his men to leave. They preceded him out the door. He stopped in front of Andrea Powell.

"My question to you stands, Mrs. Powell," he said. "How can you be with him?"

Randolph left. She heard him and his men walk across the hall and out the door. They even closed it behind them.

She stared at the five dead men piled on the floor in front of Andrew's desk and wondered what her husband had gotten them into.

TWO

Clint Adams thought about stopping off in either Tombstone or Bisbee, but there were a lot of memories there. Too many. And no friends in either place. Not anymore.

He passed through Phoenix, stopped there for one night. Phoenix was growing by leaps and bounds, had much of what towns like Denver had. Maybe, when he was done, he'd stop off there again and spend a few days.

He left Phoenix and headed for Brigham. When he got there, he put Eclipse up at the local livery, got himself a hotel room and a good meal. While he was eating, a man entered the restaurant and sat down with him.

"Mr. Adams, my name is Gordon Westin. I'm a lawyer representing Andrew Powell. Thank you for coming."

"You chose a good place to meet," Clint said. "This steak is excellent."

"We wanted to show you without delay that we can offer you good things," Westin said.

The lawyer was in his forties, a handsome man with graying black hair and a lantern jaw.

"Your meal here is on us," Westin said.

"In that case I'll have dessert," Clint said. "Care to join me?"

"Why not?" Westin said. "We still have some time before we have to go and see Mr. Powell."

Clint ordered peach pie and coffee, while the lawyer had apple.

"Can you give me some idea why Mr. Powell sent me ten thousand dollars just to come and see him?"

"I think he wants to do that himself," Westin said. "You know, when he wanted to send you that money, I told him that you don't hire out your reputation, or your gun."

"Then you must be surprised I'm here," Clint said.

"Not at all," Westin said. "Anybody can be curious."

"Especially for ten thousand dollars."

Westin smiled.

"He was going to send you five," he said. "I got him up to ten."

"Not expecting a cut, are you?"

Clint was testing Westin, who passed because he recognized that Clint was kidding.

"No," the lawyer said. "I get paid very well by Mr. Powell."

The peach pie was good, as was the coffee. They had indeed made a good choice when they told Clint to meet the lawyer at a restaurant called Lulu's.

"I suppose he has a lot of concerns in town?" Clint asked. "Maybe even owns it?"

"No," Powell said. "All of Mr. Powell's holdings are outside of town."

"I'm surprised," Clint said. "That kind of man usually spreads his money around to get himself some power in town."

"Mr. Powell is not like that," Westin said. "He lives outside of town, only comes in a couple of times a month, once to go to the bank and once to see me."

Clint finished his pie, picked up the coffeepot, and looked at Westin, who nodded. He poured the lawyer a cup, then filled his own.

"You seem to have a bad opinion of wealthy men," Westin said.

"You're right, I do," Clint said. "I've met very few rich men who don't use their money to push other people around."

"Well then," Westin said, "I think you'll be surprised when you meet Mr. Powell."

"And when will that be?"

Westin checked his watch.

"If we leave now, should be in a couple of hours."

"Let's go, then," Clint said.

The lawyer gave Clint the choice of riding his own horse, or riding in a buggy.

"Well, even though I pretty much just left him at the livery, I'd rather ride my own horse."

"Fine," Westin said. "Let's go over to the livery."

"You going to take a buggy anyway?"

"No," Westin said, "I'm glad you chose horseback. I don't get to ride as much as I'd like to."

When they reached the livery, Westin greeted the man by name.

"Mr. Adams's horse, Rusty," he said. "And I'll take my mare."

"Good," Rusty said, "she's been kinda antsy lately. Needs to take a run."

Rusty brought both horses out, stood by while both men saddled their own mounts.

"You're bringin' that big Darley back, ain'tcha?" Rusty asked hopefully.

They mounted up and Clint said, "We'll be back."

THREE

Inside of two hours they came within sight of the Powell home. There was a barn next to it, but Clint didn't see a corral.

"How can you have a ranch without a corral?" he asked Westin.

"This is not a ranch," the lawyer said. "It's just Mr. Powell's home."

"No ranch hands?"

"No."

They rode up to the house.

"I've seen homes like this in the South," Clint said, "but not many here in the West."

"Mr. Powell had it built in the Southern style," Westin said. "He actually brought the builder in from Virginia."

They dismounted. A young man came out of the barn and approached them.

"Hello, Mr. Westin," he said. He looked more like a kid though he was probably in his twenties.

"Hey, Eric," Westin said. "Can you take our horses to the barn, please?"

"Sure, Mr. Westin."

"Be careful," Clint said, handing over Eclipse's reins. "He bites."

"They all bite," the kid said. "I'll be careful."

Clint watched as the boy walked both horses away. He was surprised to see Eclipse trotting along behind him.

"He's good with horses," Westin said.

"I can see that."

"Let's go inside."

They started up the stairs.

"Is it just Mr. Powell?" Clint asked.

"No," Westin said, "there's a Mrs. Powell. You'll probably be meeting her, too."

"Does she know why I'm here?"

"She has an idea," Westin said, "although she doesn't know what it's all about."

"And you don't either?"

They stopped at the door.

"Well," the lawyer admitted, "not *all*. Only Mr. Powell knows that. Shall we go in?"

"Do we have to knock?"

"No."

"Then lead the way."

Clint followed the lawyer into the house, found himself in a large entry foyer facing a grand staircase.

"Impressive," Clint said.

"Mr. Powell's office is this way."

Westin led Clint to a room that Clint would have assumed was the living room, but instead it had been turned into a large office. A huge oak desk dominated the room, the walls of which were lined with books. There was a man seated at the desk who didn't look up when they entered.

"Mr. Pow—" Westin started, but the man held up a hand to cut him off. He was writing something and obviously wanted to finish. When he did, he put down his pen and looked directly at Clint and Westin.

"Gordon," Powell said. "Good evening."

"Sir," Westin said. "I have Mr. Adams with me."

"So I see. Welcome to my home, Mr. Adams."

"Thank you, Mr. Powell."

"Can I offer you a drink? I have some good European brandy."

"That'd be fine."

"Have a seat, please," Powell said. "Gordon, two brandies, please?"

"Yes, sir."

Clint noticed that Powell's instruction had been for two glasses of brandy, not three. He watched as the lawyer poured two, handed one to his boss, and then the other to Clint.

"Thank you, Gordon," Powell said. "That'll be all. Get yourself some coffee in the kitchen."

"Yes, sir."

Westin nodded to Clint and then left the room.

"You don't want your lawyer in on this business?" he asked.

"This is my business," Powell said, "and by that I mean personal. There's no reason for Gordon to be present."

"Well," Clint said, "that's certainly up to you."

"I truly appreciate that you came, Mr. Adams," Powell said. "Believe me, I understand that you do not hire out your gun."

"I'm here to satisfy my curiosity, Mr. Powell," Clint said.

"Not for the ten thousand dollars?"

"That helps," Clint said, "but I'm not suffering for money these days, so it's more for curiosity that I'm here."

"And why is that?" Powell asked.

"Well, if you're willing to pay me ten thousand just to come and listen to you, how much must you be willing to offer me to do whatever the job is?"

"Indeed," Powell said. "I'm willing to offer you a lot."

"We might as well get to it, then," Clint said.

"Let me do this at my own speed," Powell said.

"Sure," Clint said.

"More brandy?"

"No, this is enough."

"A few weeks ago," Powell said, "right where you're sitting now, there were five dead men piled one on top of the other."

"Five dead men?"

Powell nodded.

"They were carried in and dropped right there in front of my desk. Scared the hell out of my wife."

"Did you know the men?"

"I knew them," Powell said with a nod. "All five of them. I hired them to do a job, and that's where they ended up."

"I see."

"They were all hired for their guns," Powell said.

"Were they any good?"

"I was given to believe they were all good," Powell said. "Have you heard of Johnny Bendell or, uh, Blackie Wilcox?"

"I've heard of both of them," Clint said. "They were supposed to be pretty good."

"Well, the other men with them were apparently just as good. They all ended up dead."

"Then I guess the men they went up against were better," Clint said.

"Obviously so."

"And now you want me to go after them?" Clint asked. "Alone?"

"Whether you go alone or not is up to you," Powell said. "I simply want you to succeed where these other men failed."

"So you are trying to hire my gun."

"I'm trying to save my life," Powell said, "and perhaps the lives of my family members."

Clint leaned forward and set his empty glass on the man's desk.

"I don't think so, Mr. Powell. But thank you for the drink, and the ten thousand dollars."

As Clint stood up to leave, Powell said, "I was given to understand that one of the dead men was a friend of yours."

Clint stopped, then turned around.

"Are you playing games with me, Mr. Powell?"

"Not at all," Powell said. "The man told me he was a friend of yours when I hired him. I don't know if that was true or not."

"What was his name?" Clint aside.

"His name was Bags," Powell said. "Joe Bags. He told me that you and he were old friends. Was that true?"

"Yes," Clint said, "yes, that is true. You mind if I have another drink?"

"Not at all," Powell said. "Help yourself."

FOUR

Clint poured himself another brandy and then sat back down.

"Why would Joe Bags even mention me?" Clint asked.

"Well, he was the first one I hired," Powell said, "and he put the men together. He told me if this didn't work, that he might be able to get you to come in and take a hand."

"I see."

"Was that a lie?"

"Not a lie exactly," Clint said. "If Bags needed help with something, I might have considered it. I'm surprised, though, that he even hired out his gun. The last time I saw him, he was wearing a badge."

"Yes, I believe he mentioned that he was once a lawman."

"How did you get hold of him?" Clint asked.

"He was brought in to see me by Mr. Westin," Powell said. "He could probably tell you more."

"That might be a good idea," Clint admitted.

"I'm sure you'll find him in the kitchen if you'd like to speak to him before you make your decision."

"No," Clint said, "I think I'll go back to town and make my decision tomorrow, after I've talked with Westin and I've sent out some telegrams."

"Very well," Powell said. "I won't rush you, but I will tell you that sooner would be better than later for your decision."

"I understand that," Clint said, standing again. "I'll go and see if Westin is in the kitchen."

Powell sat back in his chair.

"I hope to see you back here tomorrow night, Mr. Adams," Powell said. "In fact, why don't you come here for dinner. You can inform my cook when you go to the kitchen to find Gordon. Her name is Chelsea."

Clint nodded, and left the office.

After a couple of wrong turns Clint found his way to the kitchen, where Gordon Westin was seated at a table with a cup of coffee in front of him. He was talking with a lovely young woman who Clint assumed was some sort of servant in the house.

"Finished?" Westin asked.

"Not quite," Clint said. "I'm going to think over Mr. Powell's offer tonight and give him an answer tomorrow."

"Really? Well, then I expect you want to get back to town." Westin stood up. "Oh, let me introduce Chelsea Piper. She's the cook here in Mr. Powell's house."

"It's nice to meet you," Clint said. "I should probably apologize, but I assumed you were a maid . . . or something."

"That's okay," she said. "It happens because I'm so young to be a cook."

"You must be a good one, to have this job," Clint said.

"She's an excellent cook," Westin said. "I've had dinner here many times."

She smiled demurely and said, "Thank you, Gordon."

"Well," Clint said, "I guess I'll get a chance to find out for myself. Mr. Powell has invited me to dinner tomorrow."

"Wonderful!" she said, clapping her hands together. "I'll try to put my best foot—or roast—forward."

"I'll look forward to it," Clint said. He looked at Westin. "Shall we go?"

FIVE

Clint and Westin rode back to town in silence. The lawyer was the first to speak when they arrived.

"I suppose you want to go right to your room?" he asked.

"Not at all," Clint said. "Let's put the horses up and go to the nearest saloon. I want to talk to you."

"As you wish," Westin said dubiously.

They hit the saloon nearest the livery, a small place with a short bar, just a few tables and only a couple of patrons. A good place to have a quiet, private talk.

They each got a beer from the bar and carried them to a table.

"What can I do for you?" Westin asked.

"You can tell me about Joe Bags," Clint said.

"What do you want to know?"

"What the hell was he doing here selling his gun?" Clint demanded.

"I don't know," Westin said. "Mr. Powell wanted me to

put out the word for guns for hire, and Mr. Bags answered the call. It was through him that we found the other men."

"But he mentioned me?" Clint asked.

"He said you and he were friends," Westin replied. "When I asked if he could get you for this job, he said perhaps later, if things didn't work out."

"So they didn't work out and he ended up dead, with all the rest of them."

"Yes."

"How many men were there altogether?"

"Five."

"Do you know how many men they were going against?" Clint asked.

"Easily five times that many," Westin said.

"Somebody's got the money to hire that many men?"

"Oh, yes."

"Why would Bags go with only five?" Clint wondered aloud.

"He seemed to think that was enough," Westin said. "I, uh, also think he only wanted to split the money five ways."

"Were you paying per man, or one lump sum?"

"One lump sum."

If Bags had hired out his gun, and then underhired because he wanted his cut to be bigger, he must have been in bad money trouble.

Clint had not heard from Joe Bags in many years, but that didn't mean the man couldn't have come to him for help.

"I'm sorry about your friend," Westin said. "Did you know the other men?"

"Powell mentioned some names," Clint said. "I knew them, but we weren't friends."

Clint got the names of the other two dead men from Westin, but he didn't know them at all.

"So what are you going to do?" the lawyer asked.

"I don't know," Clint said. "I'll have to think about it overnight, like I said. And I want to do some checking on Joe Bags. Where's he buried, by the way?"

"We gave all five of them a nice burial, outside of town."

"Were they paid in advance?" Clint asked.

"Half."

"Did you bother trying to find family to pay the other half to?"

"Uh, well, no."

"I can probably help with that," Clint said. "Powell will pay the families the other half of the money, right?"

"I suppose so."

"He'd better."

"You, uh, could make that a condition of your own employment."

"Yeah, I could," Clint said, "but I shouldn't have to."

Westin finished his beer and started to get to his feet. "All right, then. I better go back to my office and do some paperwork before I go home."

"Sit down," Clint said. "We still have some talking to do."

Westin sat back down.

"About what?"

"I think it's time you answered the main questions for me."

"And what are they?"

"What's going on?" Clint asked. "That's one."

"And the other?"

"Who's heading up this group of men that killed Bags and the other four?" Clint asked. "Who's got it in for your boss that he needs gun help?"

"Uh, I think that's for Mr. Powell to tell you."

"Well, I didn't ask him," Clint said. "I asked you."

"Um, well . . ."

"Come on, Westin," Clint said. "You represent Powell. Tell me who you guys want me to go up against."

"His name's Ben Randolph," Westin finally said.

"Ben Randolph?"

"Yes," the lawyer said. "Do you know him?"

"No," Clint said, "as a matter of fact, I've never heard of him."

Clint let Westin go back to his office while he sat and had another beer. There was no way for him to be sure that Joe Bags was, indeed, dead. He couldn't see the body because it had already been buried. All he could do was send a couple of telegrams the next morning to see what he could find out.

If he became convinced that Joe Bags had been killed by Ben Randolph and his men, then he'd have to decide if he wanted to do something about it. And if he did, did he want to take Andrew Powell's money to do the job?

None of these questions were going to be answered until morning, so he finished off his beer, stood up, and headed for his hotel.

SIX

Ben Randolph was getting impatient when there was finally a knock on his hotel room door. The town of Ariza was smaller than Brigham, a good place to hide out until his business with Andrew Powell was completed. He and his men had ridden into town and taken it completely over. The people understood they were free to go about their business, but no one was allowed to leave, and he and his men were entitled to anything they wanted.

And that included women.

Randolph opened the door and looked at the woman standing there. He'd told his number one man, Spencer, to bring him a woman who looked a lot like Andrea Powell. He thought it would give him pleasure to pretend he was fucking Powell's wife—until he could have the real thing.

This woman was tall, dark haired, slender, and had Andrea Powell's smooth, pale skin. She was also about ten years younger.

"Um, my name is Irene. They told me to come up here?" she said.

"Come in," he said.

"Can you tell me . . . why I'm here?"

"Sure," he said, "but come inside. Don't stand in the hall. People will think I'm being rude."

"Rude?" she asked, stepping inside. "You and your band of outlaws have taken over the town and you're worried about being rude?"

He closed the door and turned to face her. She was hugging her upper arms, as if she was cold.

"Have we hurt anyone?" he asked.

"N-Not that I know of."

"Well, let me assure you, we haven't," he told her. "We only need a place to stay and rest for a while, without anyone sending for the law."

"And when you're rested?"

He shrugged. "Then we'll leave."

"Is that the truth?"

"It is."

She rubbed her upper arms and looked around the room. He'd taken the biggest room in the hotel for himself.

"Well, then," she said, turning to look at him. "Why am I here?"

"I need you."

"For what?"

He studied her for a moment. She didn't seem stupid. Maybe just a bit dense at the moment.

"What do men need women for?" he asked her.

She stared at him for a few moments, then shook her head slowly and said, "Oh, no no no no . . . you don't mean . . ."

"I do mean," Randolph said. He walked up to her, his hand on her face. She closed her eyes. She didn't look like Andrea Powell, but she was certainly the same type. He rubbed his fingers over the smooth skin of her face.

"Did they tell you when they sent you over here that me and my boys get what we want while we're in town?" he asked.

"Well . . . yes, but I thought that meant . . ."

"What?" he asked, sliding his fingertips down her neck. "What did you think?"

"Well, I thought that meant . . . food, and drinks, and supplies . . . not . . ."

"Not women?"

She shook her head.

"Well, yes, that includes women." He slid one finger into the bodice of her dress, touched the smooth flesh of her breasts, and felt her shiver.

"Well then . . . you want a . . . a whore," she said with a hopeful note in her voice. "I am not a whore."

"Are you married?" he asked. "Is there a husband?"

"Well, no . . . but I'm not—"

"I'm glad you're not a whore," he said, "but don't all women want to be treated like a whore . . . sometimes?"

"I don't . . . uh, well . . ."

She was still stammering when he pulled, tearing her dress down to her waist . . .

Ten minutes later she was on her back on the bed, naked, while Randolph fucked her hard and fast. She gasped and cried out, scratched his back, drummed her heels on his naked butt, but never once did she say "no," or "stop."

Half an hour later she said, "Well, I guess you were right."

"About what?"

They were lying on their backs on the bed together, naked.

"When you said every woman likes to be treated like a whore sometimes."

"You mean you liked it?"

She slid her hand to his crotch and gripped his flaccid penis. Immediately, it began to come back to life.

"You know I did," she said. "This is a small town. There ain't nobody here like you."

"Honey," he said as she started to stroke his cock, "there ain't nobody anywhere like me."

He reached over and cupped one of her small breasts, teasing the nipple between his thumb and forefinger. She bit her lip and moaned.

"You gettin' excited again?" he asked her.

"You know I am, Ben."

"Then show me."

She smiled, slid down between his legs, started to kiss and lick his penis until it was hard. He watched the top of her head as she took him in her mouth and began to bob up and down on him. He continued to stare and pretend she was Andrew Powell's wife. Maybe he should have had the man's wife do this right in front of him that day they brought the bodies to his house. Maybe that would have taught Powell that he wasn't kidding.

He didn't know why Powell was resisting him so much. After all, it was only money.

SEVEN

Since he had eaten at only one restaurant in town, Clint went back there for breakfast. His steak and eggs were just as good as the steak dinner he'd had the night before. And the coffee was so good he had a second pot.

After breakfast he left the restaurant and started walking around town. The telegraph office in most places was found on the main street, and Brigham was no different. He had walked three blocks when he came upon the office, and stepped inside.

He had already composed both telegrams the night before, so he quickly wrote them out and gave them to the clerk. One went to Rick Hartman in Labyrinth, Texas, and the other went to Talbot Roper in Denver. Hartman and Roper were two of the smartest men he knew with the most connections, and they were two of his best friends. If anyone would have information about Joe Bags, or Ben Randolph, it would be one of them.

He told the clerk to just hold the replies for him, that he'd be checking in every hour.

* * *

He went back to walking through the town, just to get a feel of it. He turned off the main street to explore some of the side streets, and in doing so stumbled upon a shingle that said GORDON WESTIN, ATTORNEY-AT-LAW. He decided to go inside.

He opened the door and stepped in, found himself in an empty outer office that was meant for either a secretary or a receptionist. There was another closed door that said PRIVATE. He figured that was Westin's office. He was trying to decide whether to leave or knock when he heard some sounds from inside. It sounded like furniture was breaking, and then he heard a man grunt.

He rushed to the door and opened it. Inside Westin was lying on top of his desk, the legs of which had collapsed on one side. Standing around him were three men, who stopped pounding on him long enough to turn and look at Clint. They were all big, wearing trail clothes and guns, but none of them went for their iron.

"You better get out of here, cowboy," one said to him, pointing at him. "If you know what's good for you."

"You fellas need a lawyer that bad that you've got to beat one up to get him to take your case?"

"Mr. Adams," Westin gasped, "help—*oof*!" He was cut off when one of the men punched him in the stomach.

"Now, take it easy there," Clint said, taking a few steps forward.

The spokesman turned and asked him, "Are you still here?"

Clint hit him in the jaw with a right, sending him staggering back. He tripped over the damaged desk and fell over. The other two men jumped back to avoid him, then looked at Clint.

"What the hell—" one of them said.

The other one charged him. Clint sidestepped, tripped

him, and as the man went by, hit him behind the ear with a right. The attacker went down onto his face.

He turned to face the third man, who this time did go for his gun.

Clint drew. It was all he could do not to fire, though, as he rarely drew without pulling the trigger. It just didn't seem necessary this time.

"I wouldn't."

The third man stopped and stared, not believing what he'd just seen. The gun seemed to appear in Clint's hand, as if by magic.

"Damn!"

"Pick up your two friends and get out."

"Y-Yessir."

He turned to the first man, who was getting to his feet on his own. He shoved away his partner's helping hand.

"Get away from me!" he growled. "You don't know what you're doin', mister." Once again he pointed at Clint.

"Right now," Clint said, "I'm not killing any of the three of you. But that could change. Your call."

The spokesman looked at Clint's gun, then his body lost some of its tension.

"Now pick up your other friend and get out," Clint said.

The two men walked over to the third man and helped him to his feet.

"Hold it!" Clint said.

The two turned and looked at him. The third man was still dizzy, held suspended between them.

"You fellas work for Ben Randolph?"

"Who?" one of them said, looking puzzled.

Clint believed him.

"Never mind," he said. "Get out!"

They left, dragging their friend with them.

EIGHT

Clint closed the door behind them, holstered his gun, and turned to Westin, who was still lying on the broken desk.

"Are you okay?" he asked.

"Ooooh..."

Clint walked to him and helped him to his feet. He had a bloody lip and a welt above one eye.

"What happened?" Clint asked. "Who were those guys?"

"You saved me," Westin said. "They were gonna kill me!"

"I don't think so," Clint said. "I think they were just going to give you a beating."

Westin tried to straighten his tie.

"They did beat me up!" he said.

"No, I think they were going to give you a worse beating," Clint said. "If they wanted to kill you, they would have had their guns out."

"Well," Westin said, "maybe..."

"What was that about?" Clint asked. "They don't work for Randolph."

"No, I don't think so . . ."

"I know so," Clint said. "Who do they work for?"

"I don't know," Westin said. He looked around his office, which was a shambles. It looked as if they had slammed him from one end to the other before depositing him on his desk.

"What happened?"

"They came bursting in, and before I could even stand up, they dragged me out of my chair and threw me across the room. Then they grabbed me and threw me the other way. Finally, they picked me up and slammed me down on the desk and started punching me. That's when you came in."

He leaned over and studied his desk, which was not made of expensive wood.

"Damn, I'm gonna need a new desk," he said.

"A good carpenter will be able to fix that for you," Clint said. "So you don't know who they were?"

"No."

"Didn't recognize any of them?"

"No."

"And they didn't say what they wanted?"

"I told you," Westin said. "They just came in and started to beat on me."

"Without a word."

"Without a word," the lawyer said, nodding. "Anyway, thanks to you, it wasn't worse. What are you doing here?"

"I was just walking around and I saw your shingle. I thought I'd take a look and see what your office was like."

"It isn't much," Westin said.

"You must get paid enough from Powell to have a better place."

"Mr. Powell says it's not the office, but the man, that counts."

TWO GUNS FOR VENGEANCE

Westin suddenly swayed and Clint caught him and helped him to a chair.

"You want to go and see a doctor?" he asked.

"No, no, I'm fine," Westin said. "I just have a headache... and a stomachache."

"Do you keep a gun here?"

"I have one," Westin said. "It's in the bottom drawer, but I didn't have a chance to grab it. And I'm not much good with one anyway."

"Well, I'd advise you to start keeping it in your top drawer," Clint said, "that is, whenever you get your desk fixed."

Westin grinned wryly—a good sign—and said, "I'll keep that in mind."

NINE

Clint left the lawyer's office and walked back to the telegraph office.

"Got one answer for you, Mr. Adams," the clerk said as he entered. "Came in almost as soon as I sent it."

Clint assumed that it would be from Rick Hartman, and he was right. The key operator on the other side had probably run it right over to Rick's Saloon.

"Thanks," Clint said, accepting the telegram.

"Nothin' on that other one yet."

"Okay," Clint said. "I'll check back."

Clint stepped outside, then unfolded the telegram, and read. Aside from all the STOPs, it said that nothing had been heard about Joe Bags in a few years, either wearing a badge or selling his gun. Rick was sorry he couldn't be more help.

Clint folded it up and stuck it in his pocket, thinking that he, too, was sorry his friend couldn't be more help.

* * *

While waiting for the second telegram, Clint decided to go and see the local lawman. He went back into the office and asked the key operator where to find him.

"That'd be Sheriff Doby," the man said, and gave him directions.

Clint had to walk only three blocks to arrive at the sheriff's office. Doby turned out to be a big-bellied man who still wore his badge proudly after many years of upholding the law in towns across the West. He had two young deputies, who were in awe when Clint introduced himself. The sheriff sent them out to do their rounds while he talked to the Gunsmith.

"Have a seat, Mr. Adams," he said. "What can I do for you?"

"I talked with Andrew Powell last night," Clint replied, "as well as his lawyer."

"You gonna be working for Mr. Powell?" Sheriff Doby asked.

"I don't know yet," Clint said. "They told me they had some trouble at the house, and five men were killed, including a friend of mine."

"Yeah, I heard about that."

"Do you know for sure the names of the dead men?" Clint asked.

"I know what Mr. Westin and Mr. Powell told me," Doby said. He opened his top drawer and took out a sheet of paper, read off the five names Clint had already been given, including Joe Bags.

"That them?" he asked.

"Those are the names I was given also," Clint said.

"Which one was your friend?" Doby asked, putting the paper back in his drawer.

"Joe Bags."

Doby nodded, said, "I'm sorry for your loss."

"Well, I'd like to make sure there was a loss," Clint said.

"How do you mean?"

"I need to confirm that Bags was actually killed," Clint said. "I need to identify him."

"Well . . . he's already been buried, along with the others," Doby explained.

"I know that," Clint said. "Can you tell me what hotel he stayed in? Or where his possessions are?"

"Well, he and his friends stayed in the Beaufort Hotel, and I think his things are still with the undertaker."

Clint knew it was very likely the undertaker had already sold off some of Bags's possessions—his gun, his saddle. He hoped he'd be able to control his temper when he talked to the man.

"Well, I need to see something that confirms his death for me before I act," Clint said.

"Uh, and by act, what exactly do you mean?" the sheriff asked.

"What do you know about Ben Randolph?"

"I don't know anythin' about him," Doby said. "Who is he?"

"Apparently he's the man who killed Bags and his men," Clint said.

"Nobody told me that."

"What did Powell tell you?"

"Just that a group of men broke into his home and left the bodies there."

"And he said he didn't know why?"

"That's what he said."

"And you believed him?"

"Well, no . . . but what can I do about it if he doesn't want to tell me?"

"Did you talk to Mrs. Powell?" Clint asked. "I heard she was there."

"I didn't hear that either," the sheriff said. "No, I never spoke to her."

Clint frowned. What the hell was going on? Why hadn't Powell told the law the things he'd told Clint?

"So then you haven't acted on these murders?"

Doby shrugged. "I've done what I can with the information I was given," he said. "Look, Adams, I do my job—"

"Yes, yes," Clint said, "I'm sure you do, Sheriff. "It's not your fault if you don't have all the facts."

"Exactly."

Clint stood up.

"Well then, let me see if I can do something about getting you all the facts."

"What are you gonna do?" Doby asked as Clint headed for the door.

Clint stopped with his hand on the doorknob and faced the lawman.

"I guess I'm just going to have to launch a little investigation of my own."

TEN

Clint left the sheriff's office, not happy with what he had found out. For some reason Powell was keeping information from the law—information he was willing to give to Clint.

The sheriff had given him directions to both the hotel and the undertaker's office. The undertaker was closer, so he stopped there first.

The man's name was Sessions, and he had a sign in his window that proclaimed he had been in business forty years. He looked so old, though, that Clint wondered what he had done for his first thirty years.

"The sheriff told me you have the dead men's possessions, Mr. Sessions."

"Well . . . I did . . . I mean, I do, but . . ." the undertaker stammered.

Clint had introduced himself, and the undertaker had recognized his name. That was obviously why the man was so nervous.

"Look, Sessions, relax," Clint said. "I know you probably sold a lot of the things, but I'm only interested in one man. His name was Joe Bags. Do you have anything of his left?"

"Well . . . I sold his horse and saddle, but I still have his saddlebags and what was in them."

"Good. Do you still have his gun?"

"I do," the man said. "The gun belt and gun are both pretty worn, but—"

"Okay," Clint said. "Let me see what you have."

"Yessir."

He led Clint to a back room that was filled with the possessions of many dead men and women who had passed through the undertaker's hands. Clint wondered if the cluttered room was filled with items from every one of the last forty years.

"Jesus," Clint said.

"Some stuff just ain't worth sellin'," Sessions said. "I just ain't got around to throwin' it out yet."

"Where's the stuff that belonged to Bags?"

"Wait."

Sessions moved in among the mess, touched a few saddlebags, then lifted one set and turned to Clint.

"This is them."

"Are you sure?"

"Yeah."

Clint pointed a finger at him.

"Don't think you can put one over on me, old man," Clint said. "This better be his."

"It is. And so are these."

The old man turned, picked up a gun belt, and handed it to Clint. He could see what the man meant. The leather of the belt was cracked and old. The gun butt was shiny from years of wear.

"Um . . ." Sessions said.

Clint looked at him. The old man raised an eyebrow.

"You want me to pay you for this stuff?"

"Well . . . I do have to make back my investment," the man said. "I mean, five coffins—"

"I'll give you two dollars."

"Sold!"

Clint took the belt and gun and the saddlebags back to his room, where he could look everything over at his leisure.

He thought he recognized the gun as belonging to Joe Bags, but he couldn't be sure. He had an amazing memory for guns, but he had seen a lot of them over the years. He couldn't depend on that memory alone. He set the gun and belt aside.

He dug into the saddlebags. An extra shirt, another gun even more worn than the first and badly in need of cleaning, a coffeepot, a small sack of coffee, some beef jerky—he was surprised the undertaker hadn't taken the coffee and jerky—and some letters, tied together by some twine.

The letters cinched it. They were addressed to Joe Bags at a variety of different general delivery addresses in various cities or towns. The last letter had been sent to and picked up from the Phoenix Post Office. He'd read them all later, see if they had been sent by a family member. Then he'd have to notify them.

The presence of these letters in the saddlebags was not a hundred percent confirmation that the dead man was Joe Bags, but Clint figured it was about as close as he was going to get.

He packed the saddlebags back up and stuck them in a corner with the gun and gun belt. Then he left the room to return to the telegraph office to see if there was a reply from Talbot Roper.

There was.

Roper said he heard that Joe Bags hadn't been a lawman for a long time, and had taken to selling his gun. Also, he'd hooked up with some unsavory types. *Unsavory.* That was a word Roper used quite often. He usually directed it toward people he didn't like.

"Is that all ya need, Mr. Adams?" the key operator asked.

Clint had read the telegram right there in the office when the clerk gave it to him.

"Yes, that's all," Clint said. "Thanks." He turned to leave.

"That feller Bags? Mentioned in both telegrams?" the clerk said.

Clint turned back to face the man.

"You know him?"

"Not really," the clerk said, "but he was in here once to send a telegram."

"When?"

"A few days before he died."

"Who did he send it to?" Clint asked. "And where was it sent?"

The clerk hesitated. "I ain't supposed to say."

"If you weren't going to say, you wouldn't have brought it up, would you?"

The clerk looked sheepish. "No, sir."

"Then who?"

"A feller named Smith," the clerk said. "Harcourt Smith."

"You still got a copy?"

The clerk nodded. He opened a draw, brought out a copy, and handed it to Clint. It was a request for Harcourt Smith to come join Bags for a job.

TWO GUNS FOR VENGEANCE

"Did he ever get a reply?"
"No."
Clint handed the copy back.
"You know this feller Smith?" the clerk asked.
"I do," Clint said.
"What kinda feller is he?"
Clint thought for only a second, then said, "Unsavory."

ELEVEN

Clint left the telegraph office and stopped just outside. If Joe Bags had had Harcourt Smith with him, he might still be alive. The man may have been unsavory, but he was damned good with a gun.

Clint still had the hotel to check, where Bags had supposedly registered, but the clerk had given him the telegram to Smith signed by Bags. There was no longer any doubt that Joe Bags had been one of the five men killed.

Now he had to decide what he was going to do about it.

When Clint entered the sheriff's office, the man looked up from his desk at him.

"What brings you back?" he asked without a smile.

"Sheriff, I've determined to my satisfaction that my friend, Joe Bags, was one of the five men killed while working for Andrew Powell."

"Well, I'm sorry to hear that, Mr. Adams," Sheriff Doby said. "But what does that mean for you exactly? Will you be stayin' on in Brigham?"

"I still haven't decided," Clint said. "I'm supposed to have dinner out at Mr. Powell's place tonight to discuss it with him."

"But," Doby said with a frown, "you've got some questions for me first, right?"

"Well, the only information I've got about Powell comes from his lawyer," Clint said, "and he's not about to bad-mouth his client."

Doby scratched his head.

"So you think I'll bad-mouth him? Is that it?"

"No," Clint said. "I was hoping you'd be an impartial voice and tell me what you really think and know about the man."

It occurred to Clint that he should have sent telegrams to Hartman and Roper about Powell as well, but there was no time for that now. He was supposed to give the man his decision at dinner.

"I just need to know the kind of man I'd be working for if I took the job he's offering."

"Well . . . he's rich, we all know that."

"Westin told me he doesn't have much in the way of holdings in town. Is that true?"

"True enough. Mr. Powell seems to like to do his business elsewhere."

"Like where?"

"I don't know," the sheriff said. "Big towns, cities. Probably Phoenix and Denver, maybe San Francisco? He don't tell me his business."

"Do you know what business he's in?"

"He makes money," the sheriff said. "That's all I know."

"I see."

"Why don't you talk to Mr. McMillan, over at the bank?" the lawman suggested. "That's where Mr. Powell keeps his money. Maybe the bank manager knows how he makes it."

"That's actually a good idea," Clint said. He checked the clock on the wall. He had about an hour before the bank closed. He didn't know when he was supposed to go to Powell's for dinner. He'd have to depend on Westin for that.

"Thanks for your help, Sheriff."

"I didn't do much," the lawman said, "but you're welcome."

Clint nodded, turned, and left the office. He walked directly to the bank, which he had spotted earlier during his walk. It said BANK OF ARIZONA on it, which meant it was more than just a local bank.

As he entered, he saw that there were five tellers' windows—all manned—and off to one side, about four desks with people working at them. He decided to approach an attractive woman at one of the desks.

"Can I help you?" she asked as he approached. She was blond, her hair pinned tightly behind her head. She had big, beautiful eyes and a long, lovely neck. A name plate on her desk said MISS IVY.

"Yes, I'd like to speak to the bank manager, please."

"Our manager is Mr. McMillan."

"Yes, I know that," Clint said. "That's who I'd like to talk to."

"Are you sure there isn't something I could do? Or one of the tellers?"

"No," Clint said, "I need to speak with Mr. McMillan. Sheriff Doby sent me over."

"Oh!" She looked surprised. "Well, let me go and tell Mr. McMillan that you're here. What's your name?"

"Clint Adams."

Miss Ivy stood up and walked to a door just behind the tellers' windows. The suit she wore was cut severely, but did little to hide the fact that she had a long, lean, attractive body.

Clint waited, aware that the other desk workers were now looking at him. The tellers were all busy with customers. Maybe the workers thought he was going to rob the bank.

Miss Ivy came back and said, "Mr. McMillan will see you, Mr. Adams."

"Thank you, Miss Ivy."

"This way."

He followed her to the office door. She knocked, and then opened it.

"Mr. Adams, sir."

"Thank you, Miss Ivy," the man behind the desk said. "That'll be all. Will you please close the door?"

"Yes, sir."

She gave Clint a look, then backed out and closed the door.

"Mr. Adams?" McMillan stood. He was a tall man, balding, with a fringe of gray hair. He seemed to be a contemporary of Andrew Powell's. Clint wondered if they were just banker and client, or if they were friends.

"You're not one of our depositors, are you?" McMillan asked as they shook hands.

"No, I'm not."

"Please, have a seat. I understand the sheriff sent you to see me?"

"I was asking him some questions, and he suggested that you might be the man with the answers."

"Oh? What kind of questions?"

"I've been asked to work for Andrew Powell," Clint said. "I'd like to know something about the man before I agree."

"Mr. Powell is a depositor," McMillan said. "I don't think it would be appropriate for me to discuss his business."

"What about his personality?" Clint asked. "Can you discuss that?"

"Well . . . I suppose so. What do you want to know?" McMillan asked.

"What kind of man is he?"

"I don't know what you mean."

"I understand he has no holdings in town," Clint said. "I find that odd for a rich man who lives near here."

"That would be talking about his business," McMillan said, "but I will tell you this. Mr. Powell does not want to do business where he lives. He keeps his life separate from his business."

"But he has an office in his house," Clint observed.

"Well, of course," the banker said. "Most of his business is done in large towns and cities across the country. He can't go to all of them. So he has an office at home, a lawyer here in town, and he uses the telegraph office. And that is about all I'm comfortable saying."

"Is he trustworthy?"

"I have always thought him to be so. Why?"

"I have a feeling I'm not being told anything."

"Well, Mr. Adams," McMillan said, "if you're any kind of businessman yourself, you won't make your decision until you do have all the facts, will you?"

"You're absolutely right, Mr. McMillan," Clint said. "I'm having dinner at Mr. Powell's home tonight, so that's what I'm going to do." He stood up, shook hands with the man again. "Thanks for talking with me."

"Of course."

As Clint headed for the door, McMillan said, "Uh, Mr. Adams?"

"Yes?"

"You are the man they call the Gunsmith, aren't you?" the banker asked.

"Yes, Mr. McMillan, I am. Is that a problem?"

"No, no," the man said. "I was just wondering what business Mr. Powell would have with a man . . . like you."

"I'm afraid I can't discuss that, Mr. McMillan," Clint said. "Good day."

TWELVE

Clint went to his hotel and found the lawyer, Westin, waiting for him. He had a bruise over his eyes, and his lip was swollen.

"How are you doing?" Clint asked.

"Okay," Westin said. "Those men didn't come back again."

"Did you talk to the sheriff about them?"

"Uh, no, I didn't. But we can talk about that later. We have to go."

"What time are we supposed to be there?" Clint asked.

"Seven," he said. "I think we're going to be late."

"So we'll do without the buggy and go on horseback. Again," Clint said.

"Are you ready?" Westin asked.

"I assume Mrs. Powell will also be there?"

"Of course."

"Then just give me a few minutes to wash up and change my shirt," Clint said.

"I'll meet you at the livery," Westin said. "I'll have my horse saddled by the time you get there."

"Okay," Clint said, "but don't try to saddle mine or you'll lose a finger."

"Whatever you say," Westin said. "See you there."

Clint watched the lawyer leave the hotel lobby, wondering why he wouldn't report a beating to the sheriff.

He definitely wasn't being told everything he needed to know.

When he got to the livery, Westin was still cinching in his horse's saddle. It was clear he didn't saddle the animal often, and now he'd done it twice in two days. Clint quickly saddled Eclipse, and they rode out of town, heading for Andrew Powell's house.

"It'll be dark when we ride back," Clint said.

"Don't worry," Westin said, "I know the way."

"I spoke with the bank manager today," Clint said.

"Oh? About what?"

"About your boss and his business practices," Clint said.

"I didn't think Mr. McMillan talked about his clients like that."

"Don't worry," Clint said. "He doesn't."

When they reached the house, their horses were cared for by the same young man while they went inside. Clint was surprised when they were greeted by Chelsea, the cook, rather than Mr. or Mrs. Powell.

"Nice to see you again," Chelsea said.

"And you," Clint said.

"Where's Mr. Powell?" Westin asked.

"Mr. Powell is in his office, and Mrs. Powell is in the kitchen."

"Is she doing the cooking?" the lawyer asked.

Chelsea smiled. "She could, she's a good cook, but she's just supervising. I was on my way back there."

"Will you tell her we're here?" Westin asked.

"Sure."

As she left them in the foyer, Westin said, "We better let Mr. Powell know, too."

"Lead the way."

They walked to the office, probably the same route Ben Randolph and his men had walked, carrying five dead bodies—including Joe Bags.

Andrew Powell was seated behind his big desk, doing paperwork. He looked up as they entered. Clint saw the man flinch toward the top drawer of his desk, where he was keeping a gun, then relax when he saw it was them.

"Welcome," he said, standing. "I was afraid you weren't going to make it."

"My fault, sir," Clint said. "I'm sorry we're late."

"That's all right," Powell said. "You're just in time for a before-dinner drink. Brandy?"

"Sure."

"Gordon?"

"Yes, sir."

Westin moved to get the brandy, but Powell held a hand out and said, "I'll get it. You're both my dinner guests tonight."

"Thank you, sir," Westin said.

Powell poured three snifters of brandy and handed them out, keeping one for himself.

"Andrea—my wife—has been in the kitchen with Chelsea most of the afternoon. Between them I think they'll whip up quite a meal."

"I'm looking forward to it," Clint said.

"I hope you've been giving my offer some thought," Powell said.

"A lot of thought," Clint said, "and research."

"Research?"

"I needed to satisfy myself that Joe Bags was actually one of the dead men," Clint said.

"And you have?"

"Yes," Clint said. "I also needed to find out what kind of man I'd be working for if I took the job."

"And have you done that?" Powell asked.

"To some extent, yes."

"And when will you make up your mind?"

"Probably after dinner tonight," Clint said.

"Well then," Powell said, "maybe we better get to that dinner. I'll let Andrea know you're here."

"We saw Chelsea on the way in and she was going to tell Mrs. Powell."

"Well, then perhaps we should wait right here until we're summoned."

At that point Chelsea appeared in the doorway and announced, "Gentlemen, dinner is being served."

"Thank you, Chelsea," Powell said. "We'll be right there." He looked at Clint and Westin. "Well, that didn't take long, did it? Bring your brandies, gents."

THIRTEEN

The table in the dining room was long enough to accommodate a party of twenty people. It was, however, set for only four people, so only one end of the table was being used.

Powell sat down at the head of the table, instructing Clint to sit on his right and Westin on his left.

"But your wife—" Clint started.

"She'll sit there, next to Gordon," Powell said. "Don't worry, Mr. Adams, you're not taking anyone's seat."

As he said that, the door to the kitchen opened and a woman came out. Tall, slender, and extremely handsome, she looked to be in her mid- to late forties.

"Ah," Powell said, turning in his chair and then standing, "Andrea, dear. Come in and join our guests."

She approached the table and said, "Good evening, Gordon."

"Mrs. Powell."

Clint saw a look pass between the two that he was sure her husband had missed.

"Darling, this is Clint Adams, the man who is hopefully going to help us."

"Mr. Adams," she said. "Welcome."

Clint stood and said, "Thank you for the hospitality, ma'am."

Powell kissed his wife on the cheek and said, "Sit next to Gordon, my dear."

Now Clint saw something on Powell's face that he was sure his wife missed. He had the feeling he had walked into something else he didn't know or understand.

Andrea walked around and sat next to the lawyer.

"I've told Chelsea it's time—ah," Andrea said as Chelsea came through the door carrying a soup tureen.

"Ah, Andrea," Powell said. "It smells delightful, as usual."

"Thank you, sir."

They each had a soup bowl in front of them, sitting on a larger china plate. She walked around and filled each of their bowls with steaming soup.

It was just the beginning of a wonderful meal . . .

"That was an amazing meal," Clint said, sitting back in his chair.

He had just consumed as much roast beef and vegetables as he could possibly hold.

"Still dessert to come," Powell said.

"I don't know if I can manage it," Clint said, "but I'll try."

He glanced across the table at Gordon Westin and Andrea Powell, who looked extremely uncomfortable sitting next to each other.

Westin couldn't meet his eyes, but Andrea Powell stared back at him boldly.

"I understand you still haven't made your decision about working for my husband, Mr. Adams."

"No, ma'am," he said. "It's actually the reason I'm here tonight."

"Well, I wouldn't expect that decision to turn on an exquisite meal."

"It won't," he said, "but the meal certainly doesn't hurt."

"I would think not," she said. "Chelsea is a wonderful cook."

FOURTEEN

When dinner was over, Andrea stood and announced she was going to help Chelsea clean up.

"Darling," Powell said, "Chelsea is very capable of cleaning up—"

"I know that, Andrew," she said, "but what else is there for me to do? You gentlemen will now go to the den and have cigars and brandy, or whatever you want to serve. Maybe some of your wonderful scotch? What am I supposed to do? Go to my room?"

"Andrea—"

"Take your guests, Andrew," she said, shooing the men away. "Do what you have to do to get Mr. Adams to take the job you're offering him. I just hope it has something to do with all those dead men who were dumped on our floor."

"Very well," Powell said with a sigh. "Gents, accompany me to the den?"

Clint stood and said, "Mrs. Powell, please thank Chelsea for a wonderful meal?"

"I'll tell her."

"And thank you," he added. "Chelsea told us how you were helping her."

"I'm not much help," Andrea said, "but it gives me something to do."

Clint and Westin followed Andrew Powell from the room, across the foyer, and into a smaller room—Powell's den.

"Most men would have made this the office, and my office the den," he said as they entered, "but I prefer it this way. Cognac? Or would you prefer scotch, now that my wife has let the cat out of the bag?"

"Cognac is fine," Clint said.

"For me as well."

"Good," Powell said. "When it comes to my scotch, I'm an extremely selfish man."

He poured out the cognac and handed each man a small glass.

"Well now, Mr. Adams," he said, stepping back, "now that you've been well fed, what can I tell you that would help you make up your mind about this job?"

"Mr. Powell," Clint said, "I need to know why Joe Bags and those other men were killed. And why they were dumped on your floor. I need to know who Ben Randolph is, and what he has against you. Can you tell me all that?"

Powell looked at Gordon Westin.

"Gordon, why don't you go and help the ladies clear the table?" he said.

"Sir, with all due respect, that's not my job."

"With all due respect, Gordon," Powell replied, "your job is whatever I tell you your job is. Do you understand?"

"Sure, Mr. Powell," Westin said. "I understand."

"Close the doors behind you."

TWO GUNS FOR VENGEANCE 61

He left the room without meeting Clint's eyes, pulling the double doors closed.

"Have a seat, Mr. Adams," Powell said, "and I'll tell you a story."

Westin entered the dining room just as Andrea Powell was taking the last of the plates from the table.

"W-Where are they?" she asked.

"In the den," he said. "He told me to help you girls in the kitchen."

She smiled.

"Wait here."

She went into the kitchen and told Chelsea, "I'll be back in a little while."

"That's all right, Mrs. Powell," Chelsea said. "I can do the dishes."

Andrea went back into the dining room, grabbed Westin's hand, and said, "Come on."

She pulled him up the back stairs, staying away from the main stairway, down a hall, and into one of the guest bedrooms. Then she pushed him up against the wall and went to her knees in front of him. She undid his trousers, pulled them down to his ankles, then grabbed his cock, and greedily took it into her mouth . . .

"Ben Randolph and I used to be in business with each other."

"How long ago?"

"A long time."

"Okay." Clint decided to let Powell tell it in his own time.

"We were in business together years ago, and then I decided that I would be better off on my own."

"So you made yourself a fortune, and..."

"And he found me," Powell said. "Now he wants to cut himself in."

"For how much? Half?"

"All of it."

"All?"

Powell nodded.

"My cash, and my holdings."

"He doesn't want you to turn your holdings into cash?" Clint asked.

"No," Powell said, "he wants my cash, and he wants me to sign over all my holdings."

"Did you go to the law?"

"I—no, no, I didn't go to the law."

"Why not?"

"What do you want me to do, go to the local sheriff?" Powell asked. "The man's an idiot."

"How about a U.S. marshal?"

"No. Look," Powell said, "I decided to handle it myself."

"By hiring some gunmen?"

"That's right."

"Well, that didn't turn out so good for you, did it?" Clint asked.

"Not the first time."

Clint ignored that.

"What about Westin?" Clint asked. "He's your lawyer. What does he say?"

"He says what I tell him to say."

Clint stared at Powell, who was pouring himself another cognac.

"You want another?" the older man asked.

FIFTEEN

Westin was thirty-eight.

Andrea was fifty-one.

It didn't matter as much to him as it did to her.

When they first met, Westin felt a spark. He could tell she wasn't happy, and he saw the way Powell treated her. As weeks turned into months, they would talk whenever they got a chance. The one time he rode out to the house to see her, Powell wasn't around, and it happened. In the kitchen. Chelsea had the night off.

After that, they saw each other whenever they could. Stolen moments. And she always complained that she was too old for him, that he should be finding some woman his own age.

He usually used sex to shut her up.

Now they lay side by side in the guest room bed and she said, "He'll be looking for us. Both of us."

Westin rolled onto his side and put his hand over one of her breasts. She was lovely, even though she thought her body was starting to sag.

He kissed her shoulder, her neck, her nipples. She reached down and took hold of him again.

"Okay," she said, "but let's make it fast!"

"How do you expect Westin to represent you when you cut off his balls in front of people?" Clint asked.

"I don't answer to anyone about how I treat my employees," Powell said. "Believe me, I pay him enough for the opportunity to cut off his balls."

"His office doesn't look like you pay him that well," Clint commented.

Powell pointed a finger at Clint.

"He had that office when I hired him, and he chooses to stay in it. I don't know what he does with the money I pay him. He lives cheap, eats cheap, and never goes anywhere unless I'm paying the freight."

Clint couldn't argue. He didn't know enough.

"Can we stop talking about how I treat my lawyer?" Powell asked.

"Sure."

"I need you to get Ben Randolph off my back. I am not giving that man everything I've earned and built over the last dozen years."

"If I agree to work for you," Clint said, "you can't think that you're going to treat me the way you treat your other employees."

"For the amount of money I'm going to pay you," Powell said, "I'll have to trust that you know what you're doing."

"We can talk about how much you're paying me after I agree to work for you."

"And when will that be?"

Clint didn't answer.

* * *

Gordon Westin gritted his teeth as he exploded inside Andrew Powell's wife. He grunted loudly, a grunt which otherwise would have been a loud yell. When he opened his eyes and looked down at her, he could see that she was doing the same thing. Then she opened her eyes and smiled up at him.

"Jesus!" she said.

He rolled off her, trying to catch his breath. She sat up and reached for her dress.

"Now he's probably really looking for us," she said.

He reached to the floor for his clothes.

"I'll tell him I was outside, walking," he said. "After the way he spoke to me in front of Adams, he'll believe me."

"I'll think of something," she said.

He watched as she stood up, turned her back to him, and slid her dress over her head. He felt a sense of loss when the dress covered her naked back and ass.

He knew he could not ask her to leave Powell until he had something to offer her. That was why he spent very little of the money her husband paid him. He saved it. He'd never have as much as Powell, but maybe someday he'd have enough to be able to take her away from him.

She turned and looked at him.

"I'll go down first."

"All right."

"But before that," she said, touching her messed-up hair, "I have to find a mirror."

She kissed her fingertips and waved to him, then slipped out of the room.

"Mr. Adams," Powell said, "I realize that you could go after Ben Randolph and his men to find out who killed your friend, and you could do it on your own."

"And?"

Powell shrugged.

"I just assumed you'd rather do it and get paid for it," Powell said. "A lot!"

Clint thought a moment, then said, "I'll have another cognac, Mr. Powell."

SIXTEEN

"Ah, Gordon," Powell said as the lawyer walked back into the den, "have you seen my wife?"

Seen her, Westin thought, and had her, you old bastard.

"I think she's back in the kitchen, with Chelsea," Westin said. "I was . . . outside. Walking."

"Uh-huh," Powell said, obviously not interested.

"Well," Powell said, "I think the ladies will have coffee for us. And pie. I'll go and check. Gordon, why don't you stay here and talk to Mr. Adams."

"Yes, sir."

"Answer whatever questions he has," Powell added. "I think he'll make his decision tonight, before you and he leave."

"Yes, sir."

Clint and Westin watched as Powell left the room.

"Why do you put up with him?" Clint asked.

"He pays well."

"But he treats you like shit."

"And pays me well for the privilege."

"Why don't you have a better-looking office, then?" Clint asked.

"What does that matter?" Westin asked. "All I need is a desk."

"So . . . you're saving your money?"

Westin walked to the cognac and poured himself one.

"That's right. And when I have enough money, I'll tell the old buzzard where to go."

"Sounds like a good plan."

"Are you going to work for him?"

"Well, one way or another I'm going to find out who killed Joe Bags and those other men," Clint said. "So I might as well let him pay me while I'm doing it."

"Kind of sounds like what I'm doing," Westin said. "Using the old man to get what I want."

Clint hesitated, then said, "His wife?"

Westin almost choked on his cognac. He took a quick look at the door.

"What—why—how—"

"I saw the way you were looking at each other at dinner," Clint said.

"Jesus," Westin said. "Oh, Jesus. Do you think he knows—"

"No," Clint said, "I don't think he ever looked at either of you enough to see it. How long has it been going on?"

"Um, almost a year," Westin said. "Since we first met."

"So that's what you're saving your money for, then?" Clint said. "You think she'll leave him when you have enough?"

"I hope so," Westin said. "You—uh, you're not going to say anything to Mr. Powell, are you?"

"Why would I say anything?" Clint asked. "It's none of my business."

"I just thought maybe, when you were working for him, you might feel obligated—"

"I won't feel any obligation beyond what he's paying me to do."

"So you are going to take the job?"

"I suppose so," Clint said, "but I think I'll hold off telling him until after dessert."

"Sounds like a good idea to me."

Clint slapped Westin on the back.

"You might want to be careful with those looks you and Mrs. Powell have been giving each other, though."

"I'll keep that in mind," Westin said.

Dessert was as good as the rest of the meal, except Clint felt he might have been getting more attention from Chelsea than he was getting before. He was getting looks, and an occasional hip bunt, the kind he'd experienced before from waitresses who were interested in him.

He didn't know much about Chelsea beyond the fact that she cooked for the Powells. He didn't know where she lived, or what her situation was.

Chelsea's attentions were distracting him from watching Westin and Mrs. Powell, but the lawyer did seem to be showing more sense when it came to casting hot and wanting looks her way.

"Well, Mr. Adams," Powell said, sitting back in his chair and wiping his mouth with a cloth napkin, "what do you say?"

"I say okay, Mr. Powell," Clint said. "I'll take your money while I'm looking for the killer of Joe Bags."

"I've told you who the killer is," Powell said. "Ben Randolph."

"I'd like to know who pulled the trigger," Clint said.

"And to get started, I'll need you to tell me where to find Randolph."

"Well, I don't know that."

"Then where are you supposed to get in touch with him? I mean, if you wanted to make arrangements to pay him off?"

Clint looked at Mrs. Powell, to see if he'd let the cat out of the bag.

"That's all right, Mr. Adams," she said. "I'm well aware of what's going on. After all, I watched five dead men get dropped on the floor of my house. After that, I insisted on knowing everything that was going on."

Clint looked at Powell. He wondered if the man had really told his wife everything.

"Ben said he'd be coming back here," Powell said.

"Did he say when?"

"No."

"Then how am I supposed to know—"

"How about this?" Powell asked. "Do you have a hotel room?"

"I do."

"Well, give it up and stay here," Powell said. "You'll be our houseguest until Ben Randolph shows up again."

"And then you can kill him," Andrea said.

All the men at the table turned and looked at her. Even Chelsea stopped and looked.

SEVENTEEN

"Mrs. Powell," Clint said. "I am not being hired to kill Ben Randolph."

"Then I'm confused," she said. "Aren't you a hired gunman? Isn't that what you do?"

Clint sat back in his chair and looked at Chelsea. The cook put her hand over her mouth and stared back at him. He didn't think she was judging him. Rather, he thought she was feeling sorry for him.

"That'll be all, Chelsea," Powell said. "You can finish cleaning the kitchen tomorrow. You can go to your room."

"Yes, sir."

They all remained silent until Chelsea had left the room.

"Andrea—" Powell said.

"Mrs. Powell—" Clint started.

They both stopped.

"Do you mind?" Clint asked Powell.

"No," the man said. "Go ahead. Please."

"Mrs. Powell—"

"If you're about to scold me," she said, holding up her hand, "I'd prefer you call me Andrea."

"Andrea," he said. "One of the men your husband hired was a friend of mine. My only interest is in finding out who killed him and bringing that man to justice. If I can do something for your husband to help him with his Ben Randolph problem, I will. That might mean killing someone, but only if I have no other choice. I don't hire out to kill people."

"I'm sorry," Andrea said. "I didn't mean to insult you."

"That's okay."

"So what about it, Clint?" she asked. "Will you stay as our guest?"

"That seems to be the way to do this," Clint said. "I'll go back tonight—"

"Nonsense," Powell said. "We have plenty of rooms in this house. You and Gordon will stay the night, and then he can go back to town tomorrow, check you out of the hotel, and bring your things here. That way you'll be here tonight and tomorrow . . . uh, just in case Ben returns."

Andrea stood up.

"I better see to your rooms," she said to Clint and Westin.

It seemed to Clint she was happier about Westin staying than about him.

When Clint's room was ready, Andrea Powell came into the dining room to get him.

"Your room is ready," she said. "I'll show you where it is. After that, you may do as you like, remain in it, or wander the house."

"If it's all right with you," Clint said to Powell, "I'd like to look at that library of books you have in your office."

"You're a reader?" Andrea asked, showing her surprise.

"That shocks you?"

"Yes—well, no—I mean—"

"That's all right, Andrea," Clint said. "I realize it will take you some time to get rid of your view of me as a gunman. Shall we go?"

Sheepishly she led him from the dining room and up the stairway, leaving her husband and her lover at the dining room table alone.

"What do you think?" Powell asked the lawyer.

"About what?"

"Don't be dense, man," Powell said. "Can he get the job done?"

"I'm sure he can."

"Alone?"

"That'll be up to him," Westin said. "I imagine he could get a lot of help if he wanted to."

"Help like Wyatt Earp and Bat Masterson?"

"We know that he is friends with those men," Westin said, "but I doubt they would be interested in this particular job. But whoever he brings in, you'll have to pay for."

"Why can't he pay them from what I'm giving him?" Powell asked.

"Perhaps that should have been ironed out ahead of time."

"Well . . . we haven't really settled on an amount," Powell said.

"Then there's still room to negotiate," Westin said.

"Perhaps we can get that done tomorrow," Powell said.

"Perhaps we can," Westin agreed.

* * *

Andrea showed Clint to a guest room that was twice the size of his hotel room.

"Wow," he said. "Very impressive."

"My husband had the house built, but I furnished it," she said. "All the rooms but his office."

"You have good taste."

"Would you like me to find you something to sleep in?" she asked.

"No, that's fine. I'll manage."

"I can find you a shirt for tomorrow."

"That would be nice, thank you."

When she hesitated to leave, he knew what was coming.

"Mr. Adams . . . he and I haven't talked about it, but I suspect you know about me and . . . Gordon."

"I suspected," Clint said, "but as I told Gordon, it's not my place to say anything."

A look of relief came over her face.

"Thank you," she said. "I appreciate that."

"As I told Westin," Clint said, "just be careful around your husband. If he stops to take a good look, he might see what I saw."

"We'll remember that," she said. "Good night. I won't see you again until morning."

"Good night, Andrea. Thank you for your hospitality."

EIGHTEEN

Clint waited about half an hour, giving everyone time to get away from the dining room, off to wherever they were going. When he finally went back downstairs, he hoped he wouldn't find Powell sitting at his desk in his office. He was in luck—the room was empty.

He went into the room and started browsing the books. There was a lot of nonfiction, history books, except for one wall, which was fiction. A lot of it was fiction he didn't recognize, but he did see Mark Twain, Robert Louis Stevenson, Charles Dickens, and others he knew and had read.

"Impressed?"

He turned at the sound of a woman's voice, was surprised to see Chelsea standing in the doorway. She had removed her apron and was wearing a simple cotton dress. The green of the dress went well with the red of her hair.

"Yes, I am," he said. "Do you spend any time in here?"

"I'll tell you," she said, "if you promise not to tell anyone."

"I promise."

"I come in when nobody's around, and read the books," she confessed.

"Do you ever take a book with you to read?" he asked.

"Oh, no," she said. "Mr. Powell would notice if a book was missing."

"Really? With all these books?"

"Oh, yes," she said. "He has that type of mind. He sees everything."

"Everything?"

"Well," she said, "not everything." She looked behind her, to make sure no one was within earshot, then came farther into the room. "He doesn't see what's going on between his wife and his lawyer."

"But you do?"

"Oh, yes," she said, her eyes wide. "Can I tell you another secret?"

"Please do."

"I saw them, the very first time they were together," she said. "They didn't think anyone was around, but I was."

"And they did it where you could see them?" he asked.

"Well, yes," she said, "considering they were doin' it in my kitchen!"

"And you watched?"

"From the cupboard," she said. "It was funny, but do you know watching two people have sex is not a pretty sight? I finally had to close the door and just wait there until they finished."

"So you never told Mrs. Powell you saw them?"

"Oh no," she said, "I don't know who would die of embarrassment more, her or me."

"Probably her."

Chelsea giggled behind her hands. In her mid-twenties, she was still able to do that and carry it off as cute.

"What are you going to read?" she asked, putting her hands behind her back.

"I don't know," he said. "I thought I might take something up to my room, but after what you just told me . . ."

"Oh, I wouldn't," she said. "Not without asking Mr. Powell first."

"Well, maybe I'll just pick out a book and sit in here and read it," Clint said. "He's not coming back down here, is he?"

"I don't think so," she said. "Not tonight. But he'll be down early in the morning. He's always early."

"Okay, thanks for the tip."

"I know where your room is," she said.

He looked at her. He couldn't tell anything from the expression on her face.

"Do you want to know where mine is?"

"Sure."

"It's at the end of the same hall," she said. "Come out of your room, turn right, and it's at the end of the hall on the right. That's me. I mean, just in case you need something. You don't want to have to wake Mr. and Mrs. Powell."

"They sleep in the same room?"

"Yes, they do," she said. "As far as he knows, she's his happy wife."

"Knowing what you know must stretch your loyalty," Clint said. "I mean, he pays you, but you're around her all the time . . ."

"Believe me," she said, "they both treat me like an employee. There's no question of loyalty."

He nodded his understanding.

"Well," she said, backing toward the door, "I guess I'll let you find your book."

"Okay."

"Will you be down here long?" she asked. "I mean, reading?"

"I don't know," he said. "Probably not too long."

"Okay," she said. "I'll see you . . . later."

She left him standing there, wondering if she was trying to tell him what he thought she was trying to tell him.

NINETEEN

Clint was sitting in a comfortable armchair, leafing through a book on European history, when Gordon Westin came walking in.

"Making yourself comfortable?" the lawyer asked.

"Yes," Clint said.

Westin walked to the sideboard, where Powell kept his liquor.

"Cognac? Or whiskey?" he asked.

"Cognac," Clint said. "I'm more of a beer man than a whiskey man, but I like a good cognac."

Westin poured out two snifters, handed one to Clint, who set the book down on the table next to the chair.

"The boss won't mind if us lowly peons drink his liquor?" Clint asked.

"What he doesn't know won't hurt him," Westin said.

The lawyer sat in another armchair, across from Clint, crossed one leg over the other.

"Mr. Powell has authorized me to discuss your fee," he said.

"I'll tell him what my fee is," Clint said. "If he doesn't pay it, I'll just go ahead without him."

"Well, you've been decent to me and to Andrea about . . . what's going on," Westin said. He looked around to make sure no one was listening. "You tell me how much you want, and it's a done deal."

Clint studied the young man for a few moments, then said a number.

"Done."

"Are you serious?"

"Powell's got more money than God," Westin said. "I'll tell him we haggled."

Westin stood up and extended his hand. Clint stood up and took it.

"What about other men?" Westin asked.

"Do we know how many men Ben Randolph has with him?" Clint asked.

"Twenty, maybe twenty-five."

"Then I might need some help," Clint said. "Powell would have to pay them, too. Is that a problem?"

"Not for me," the lawyer said, "but they won't get what you get."

"That's no problem," Clint said.

"Then we're set."

"You sure you don't want something in return?" Clint asked.

"Like what?"

"A percentage?"

"I think you know what I want, Clint," Westin said. "Your fee is all yours."

They finished their drinks. Westin wiped the glasses as clean as he could and put them back.

"I think I'll be turning in," he said to Clint. "Enjoy your book."

"Thanks."

Westin headed for the door, and Clint sat back down and picked up the book.

"By the way," Westin said at the doorway.

"Yeah?"

"Watch out for Chelsea."

"What do you mean?"

"I think she likes you," he said with a smile. "And she's pretty aggressive."

"Thanks for the warning."

"The master bedroom is at the other end of the house," Westin said, "so don't worry about making too much noise."

"I'll see you at breakfast," Clint said.

"Good night."

Clint finished leafing through the book about an hour later and returned it to the shelf. He left empty-handed and went to his room. He wondered if Chelsea was aggressive enough to be waiting there, but when he walked in the room, the bed was empty.

He closed his door tightly, pulled off his boots, and looked for someplace to hang his gun belt where it would be within easy reach.

TWENTY

Clint went to bed thinking about Chelsea. She was young and pretty, had been wearing an apron most of the times he saw her. But when she came into the office wearing only a dress, he could see she had a nice body. Her hair was red, her eyes green, always a good combination.

He rolled over in bed, wondering if he would be overstepping his bounds, taking advantage of his host by going down the hall to Chelsea's room. But hadn't she invited him? Or had he misread her?

He didn't think that was the case. After all, hadn't Westin told him she was aggressive? And she was too good at her job to have been accidentally hip-bumping him all through dinner.

His other problem was, if he did go down the hall, did he bring his gun with him? What if he was in Chelsea's room when Ben Randolph and his men showed up? If he came to Chelsea's room with his gun, she'd just have to understand.

He grabbed his gun belt, slung it over his shoulder, and left the room to creep down the hall.

* * *

In his own room, Gordon Westin slowly undressed. This was the first time his boss had ever asked him to stay overnight, and he wasn't comfortable. Was it only because of Clint Adams's presence, or did Powell suspect something going on between him and Andrea?

Westin had a gun, although he wasn't very good with it. It was small caliber and he carried it in his jacket pocket. Before turning in, he placed it under his pillow. He hoped he wouldn't shoot himself in the head during the night.

Andrea Powell slept fitfully next to her husband. Usually she slept well enough, but tonight her lover was under the same roof with her husband. Westin's presence made her nervous. She knew it was due to the fact that her husband wanted Clint Adams to stay, but what if he also suspected something?

She was afraid to sleep, fearing her husband would rise and do something foolish.

In her room, Chelsea Piper waited. Had she been obvious enough for Clint Adams? If he didn't come, she was going to feel silly going to sleep in her flimsy nightgown.

She'd heard stories about Clint Adams, that he killed men and loved women. She knew he was there to kill men, but she was hoping she could convince him to give her some time.

It had been a while for her. She didn't meet many men working and sleeping in Andrew Powell's house. Westin might have been a possibility, but he took up with the boss's wife. And the men she met the few times she went into town were filthy and mannerless.

She sat on her bed, waiting. As time went by, she started

to feel foolish, but then a floorboard creaked out in the hall. She waited, listening, then heard some other boards. She knew from experience that someone was walking down the hall.

She kept herself from getting to her feet and moving to the door. If there was a knock, she did not want to seem too anxious.

But when the knock came, very gently, she hurried barefoot to the door, waited a moment, and then opened it a crack.

TWENTY-ONE

The door opened a crack and Chelsea looked out.

"Mr. Adams," she said. "Do you always creep around at night?"

"I was under the impression I was invited," he said. "Was I wrong?"

She hesitated a moment, possibly not wanting to seem too anxious, then said, "No, you weren't wrong." She opened the door wide. She was wearing a flimsy nightgown that clung to her, revealing full breasts with large nipples, and a dark pubic patch. "Come in."

He entered and she closed the door gently, then turned to face him.

She smiled and said, "You could have stolen a bottle of the boss's whiskey."

"Will we need it," he asked, "to get into the mood?"

"Well," she said, "I won't."

She approached him, put her arms around his neck, yanked him down, and kissed him soundly.

They kissed for a long time and then she held him at arm's length and asked, "Too bold?"

"No, no," he said, gathering her back in, "it's just fine."

He kissed her again, and when they came up for air, she was gasping.

"Oh my . . ." she said.

He let her go and she backed away, her breasts heaving. Her nipples had hardened and there was a damp patch between her legs. She might as well have been wearing nothing.

She seemed to notice his gun belt for the first time.

"Did you really think you'd need that?" she asked.

He took the belt from his shoulder.

"You never know," he said. "I just like to be prepared."

"I suppose that's the way a man like you must live."

He walked to her bed, hung the belt on the bedpost. When he turned to face her, she had removed her nightgown and let it fall to the ground. Now he could see every pale inch of her. The space between her lovely breasts was spattered with freckles, and the thatch of hair between her thighs was a darker red than the hair on her head—almost copper.

Andrea listened to the deep breathing of her husband. She knew from experience that he slept very soundly. Did she dare sneak from the bed, the room? If he caught her, she could say she was going down to the kitchen to make herself a cup of tea.

Slowly, carefully, she pushed the cover down and slipped from the bed. She stood next to it a moment, but her husband's breathing never varied. She grabbed her robe, donned it, and padded barefoot to the door. She opened it silently, stepped out into the hall, and then closed it quietly.

She started down the hall, but saw ahead of her, at the

far, far end of the hallway, that someone was walking. She stopped. It was Clint Adams, and he was walking away from her, and so he didn't see her. He stopped at a door and knocked. Andrea held her breath, hoping he wouldn't look her way.

He was admitted to the room, leaving her alone in the long hallway. She made her way as far as his door. That was as far as she needed to go to see that he had entered Chelsea's room. Well, why not? She was young and pretty, and he was a handsome man. Why shouldn't they spend a night together?

Between his door and Chelsea's door was the room that Gordon Westin was in. She had two choices. She could knock on his door, or she could actually go downstairs and have a cup of tea.

After struggling with herself, she decided to go down and have the tea.

Gordon Westin rolled around on the bed restlessly, finally got to his feet, and paced. If he'd been a smart man, he would have taken up with the cook, Chelsea, and not with the lady of the house. Then he could have just walked down the hall to her room. This way, knowing that Andrea was only doors away, he couldn't sleep.

He put on a robe that Andrea had given him, belted it around his waist, and left the room. As he did, he thought he heard someone going down the stairs. He moved to the head of the stairs and saw Andrea reach the bottom. He stepped back, in case she looked up, and he wondered where she was going. Maybe she was as restless as he was?

Maybe she was gong to the kitchen, where they had first started their relationship.

He waited a few moments, then went down the stairs.

TWENTY-TWO

Clint removed his boots and shirt but Chelsea became impatient with him and started tugging at his belt. She pulled his trousers and underwear down and he kicked them away. His penis was already hard and she fell onto it, dropping to her knees and taking it in her hands. She rubbed the hot column of flesh over her cheeks, rolled it between her hands, wet the tip with her lips and tongue. She ran her tongue up and down it, wetting it before finally taking it into her mouth.

She moaned as she began to suck him, and he groaned and rose up onto his toes in response to the suction of her mouth.

He placed his hands on her head as she continued to bob up and down on him.

Andrea had a pot filled with water on the stove, and was just lighting it when Gordon Westin walked in. She jumped.

"Gordon. You startled me."

"I'm sorry," he said. "I was . . . restless."

"I was just going to put on a pot for tea. Would you like some?"

"As a matter of fact, I would."

She took the pot to the pump, added more water, then placed it on the stove and lit it.

Westin sat at the table and watched her work, pretending she was his, that they were living together in this house. It was a nice fantasy.

She turned, smiled when she saw him watching her, then sat across from him at the table.

"What if your husband comes down?" he asked.

"What if he does?" she asked. "All we're doing is having tea."

"Yes," he said, "we are just having tea. But I remember a day we did something else in this kitchen."

She blushed and said, "That was foolish. We took a big chance that day."

"Are you sorry?" he asked.

"No," she said, "I'm not sorry."

He reached over and took her hands in his.

Clint took hold of Chelsea by her upper arms and lifted her to her feet. He kissed her mouth, her neck. The freckles between her breasts, and then her breasts and nipples. She shivered as he bore her down to the bed.

They pressed together and her skin burned him. He loved hot women—women whose very bodies seemed to generate their own heat.

He slid a hand down between her legs, found her slick and wet. He rubbed her, kissed and sucked her nipples until she began to tremble. Then he slid down between her legs and began to lap at her, licking her up and down while she squirmed and gasped.

* * *

Andrew Powell turned over in bed and noticed that his wife's side was empty. He placed his hand on the sheet. It was still warm from her. Most likely she couldn't sleep and had gone downstairs for some tea. He closed his eyes and fell back to sleep, because the last thing he suspected was that his wife would ever be with another man.

He never gave it a thought.

In the kitchen Westin and Andrea sat with their cups of tea and talked. They held hands across the table, but always ready to pull their hands back at a moment's notice—like if they heard footsteps in the dining room.

"I don't know how much longer I can do this," she said. "And then there's Ben Randolph. I don't know the whole story there, Gordon. Do you?"

"No," he said. "Your husband keeps it to himself. I know they have a history together, and for some reason, Randolph thinks your husband owes him. But I don't know why."

"Do you think Mr. Adams can solve the problem?" she asked.

"If he can't, I don't think anyone can," he said.

"And if he can't?"

"Then, if your husband doesn't pay him, he'll probably kill him."

"Kill Andrew?"

Westin nodded.

Andrea squeezed his hand and asked guiltily, "And would that be so bad?"

TWENTY-THREE

Ben Randolph finished his drink, picked up the bottle, and found it empty. Just as well. Time to turn in. It was getting late and the next day would be a big one.

He was about to get up from his table in the saloon when three of his men walked in—Lane Barrett and two others. He waited while they each got a beer and then walked over to his table.

"Want a drink, Ben?" Barrett asked.

"Nope," Randolph said. "I just finished and was headed to bed. You boys ought to do the same. We got a big day tomorrow."

"So tomorrow's it, huh?" Lane asked. "The day we collect?"

"That's right."

"You mind if I sit a minute?"

"A minute's all you got."

Lane jerked his head at the other two men, who reluctantly withdrew to the bar. Lane sat down across from Randolph. The gang leader remembered that Lane Barrett and the other two had joined him at the same time. The three of them always stuck together.

"Me and the boys been wonderin'," Lane said.

"Wonderin' what?"

"About the money."

"There'll be plenty of money."

"Yeah, but there's . . . what? Twenty-five of us? How you gonna pay us all off?"

"Don't you worry about that, Lane," Randolph said. "That's my problem."

"Well . . . I was just tryin' to be helpful to ya, Ben," Lane said.

"In what way?"

"Well, I was thinkin', ya really don't have to pay off *everybody*, do you?"

"Well," Randolph said, "I don't have to pay everyone the same amount."

"We was thinkin' of not payin' some people at all."

"And who were you thinkin' of leavin' out?" Randolph asked.

"Mostly we been thinkin' of who to leave in," Lane explained.

"The three of you, of course."

"Yeah," Lane said, "and a few of the others. I mean, we're gonna do most of the work. We're the ones who killed those five hired guns the old man sent after you."

"That's true."

"And you can count on us."

"That's true, too."

"So it's better to pay off seven maybe eight men, and not the rest."

"And what do we do with the rest?" Randolph asked.

"Well, that's up for discussion."

"We can't run out on them," Randolph said. "Although if we did, I'm the one they'd go lookin' for."

"Well, yeah . . ."

"You weren't worried about that, were you?"

"We'd back ya, Ben," Lane said. "No worries there. Of course, we could kill 'em all."

"In their sleep?"

"That's one way."

"That's kind of bloodthirsty, isn't it, Lane?" Randolph asked.

"Just money hungry, Ben," Lane said. "If we can figure out a way to do it without killin' them, I'm all for it."

"I tell you what," Randolph said. "I'll give it some thought."

"Sure, sure," Lane said, "you do that."

"Now I'm going to turn in. See you in the morning, at the livery, like we planned."

"Sure, Ben," Lane said. "We'll meet ya there. Good night."

Randolph stood up, didn't looked at the men standing by the bar, and left the saloon.

After Randolph was gone, the other two men joined Lane Barrett at the table.

"What'd he say?" Horace Brandt asked.

"He's gonna think about it."

"You think he really will?" Abner Grant asked.

"It don't matter," Lane said. "Whether he goes for the idea or not, we're gonna end up with all that money."

"How many we got backin' us?" Abner asked.

"Five," Lane said. "The eight of us can handle the rest."

"And then what?" Brandt asked.

Lane looked at them both. "Then we'll handle the other five. We're gonna split a helluva lot of money three ways, boys."

TWENTY-FOUR

Clint slid his penis into Chelsea's vagina, taking his time, enjoying the feel of her heat engulfing him. When he was all the way in, he started moving, slowly at first, then faster and faster. She gasped, moving her hips to keep up with him. He had her on her back with her knees raised, spread wide. They made wet, sucking noises as they strained against each other, and did their best to keep their gasps and grunts quiet.

"Oooh, Jesus," she said, hooking her arms behind her knees to keep her legs up.

Clint continued to listen for sounds outside in the hall as he fucked her, but eventually she took all of his attention. At one point the only way they would have heard anyone was if the intruder had kicked the door open.

"Oh, yeah," she said, "it's been a long time, but I don't remember it ever being this good."

"It should always be this good, Chelsea," he said. "Always."

She sighed, and closed her eyes, giving herself up to the sensations . . .

"What do you have on under that robe?" Andrea asked Gordon Westin.

"Never mind," he said.

"Don't you want to know what I have on under my gown?" she asked, standing.

"Andrea—"

She shrugged, and her nightgown fell to the floor, leaving her gloriously naked in the middle of the kitchen.

Westin caught his breath as he looked at her. She complained about her age, and the condition of her body, but he thought she was beautiful.

"Andrea—"

"He's asleep," she said, putting her hand to the side of his face.

"But—"

She knelt in front of him and reached into his robe, into his underwear, and drew out his stiff penis. Laughing to herself, she fondled it while he opened his robe fully, and she then took him in her mouth.

In the kitchen, he thought . . . again.

"I should go back to my own room," Clint said later. Chelsea was lying in the crook of his arm. She turned her head up to look at him.

"Why?"

"I'm a guest here," he said. "I don't want to be caught sneaking out of your room in the morning."

"We have time before the household wakes up," she said. "I have to be in the kitchen early to make breakfast, so you'll be out of here in plenty of time."

"Are you sure?"

"I guarantee it," she said, turning so that her breasts were pressed up against him. "There's something else I can guarantee you, too."

"And what's that?"

She slid her hand down between his legs and said, "I can guarantee you a good time if you stay."

She squeezed him, then stroked him while kissing the side of his neck.

"Well," he said, sliding his hand down her back to the crease between her butt cheeks, "if you guarantee it . . ."

Early the next morning a rider entered town, rode down the street, and stopped at the hotel.

"Can I help you?" the clerk asked. "Kinda early to be ridin' into town."

"I rode all night," the man said. "Can I get a room?"

"Sure thing." The clerk turned the register book around so the man could sign in. The stranger signed his name, then stopped when he noticed the name above his.

"Is this man still here?" he asked, pointing.

"Mr. Adams? He's still registered, but at the moment he's not in the hotel."

"Where is he?"

"Uh, I think he went out to see Mr. Powell last night, and he ain't come back yet."

"What about a man named Joe Bags?"

"I don't know that name."

The stranger nodded, turned the book back around to the clerk, and accepted his key.

"Thanks. I'm gonna take care of my horse and then come back."

"Yes, sir. The livery is right down the street."

"Obliged," the man said, and left.

The clerk looked down at the book, read the name: *Harcourt Smith*.

He didn't know the name, and closed the book.

TWENTY-FIVE

Clint succeeded in getting out of Chelsea's room and back to his own without being seen. Chelsea went downstairs to prepare breakfast for everyone.

Andrea and Westin had gotten back to their rooms the night before, also without running into anyone. Westin slept well, while Andrea still slept fitfully next to her husband, who was fast asleep.

Powell woke refreshed for the first time in weeks. Having Clint Adams in the house was a good tonic for him.

When Clint got down to the dining room, Powell was already there, having coffee.

"Good morning," Clint said.

"Morning," Powell said. "Did you sleep well?"

"Very well, thanks."

"Coffee's right there on the sideboard. Help yourself."

Clint walked over and poured himself a cup, carried it back the table.

"I was thinking," he said, "that I'd go into town with Gordon and pick up my things."

"I don't think that's a good idea," Powell said. "Randolph and his men might show up today. Gordon can get your stuff. Do you have a particular reason for wanting to ride in?"

"Do you have a particular reason for not wanting me to go?"

"Well . . ."

"You know when Randolph is coming back, don't you?" Clint asked.

Powell didn't answer.

"Damn it—"

"Okay, okay," Powell said, "I'll increase your fee. Just don't . . . change your mind, but . . ."

"Today?" Clint asked incredulously. "He's coming back today?"

"To talk," Powell said. "Just to talk. All I want is for you to stand next to me."

"And if lead starts flying?"

"You know better than me what to do if that happens," Powell said.

"Goddamnit, Powell—"

Clint stopped when Andrea Powell entered the room.

"Don't stop scolding him on my account, Clint," she said.

Clint got up to pour coffee for Andrea. As he was doing that, Gordon Westin entered.

"What about you?" Clint asked. "Did you know Randolph was supposed to be coming back today?"

Westin stopped in his tracks, as if he'd been slapped.

"What? No!" Westin looked at Powell. "How's he supposed to get any help?"

"Look, once Randolph knows the Gunsmith is backing me, he'll back down."

"You think so?" Clint asked, placing Andrea's coffee in front of her. "What if he just comes back with more men?"

"Well, if he comes back today and sees that you're here, we'll all know what he intends to do."

"And maybe we'll all just end up dead," Clint said. "Powell, I think your wife should go back to town with Gordon."

"That's probably a good idea," Powell agreed. "Dear, why don't you pack a bag and go with Gordon? You can stay in town until this blows over."

"You think this is just going to blow over?" she asked. "Really?"

"Well . . . then stay until it's over."

"And if you die out here while I'm in town?" she asked.

"Then you'll be a wealthy widow."

She stood up, her eyes flashing.

"That's not funny, Andrew!"

She stormed out of the room, presumably to pack a bag.

"Take her with you, Gordon," Powell said.

"Yes, sir."

"Take everything from Clint's room, then come back without her."

Westin nodded.

The door to the kitchen opened and Chelsea entered carrying a plate full of flapjacks.

"You can leave right after breakfast," Powell added.

"Yes, sir."

The three men enjoyed their flapjack breakfast while Andrea Powell packed her bag. On the one hand, she was angry at her husband for sending her away. On the other hand, in town she would have more time to spend with Gordon Westin.

TWENTY-SIX

Ben Randolph awoke that morning, rolled Irene off his outstretched left arm without waking her. From behind she still looked quite a bit like Andrea Powell. Well, maybe she didn't look like her, but she certainly reminded him of her.

He swung his legs to the floor and stood up. Naked, he walked to the window and stretched, then looked out. He couldn't see the livery stable from where he was, but knew his men would be gathering there.

Lane Barrett was going to be a problem. If he got enough men to follow him, they might even try to take the money away. His proposal of getting rid of most of the men after they got the money was a good one, but it also meant he was ambitious.

There was nothing worse than an ambitious thief.

Irene moaned and rolled onto her back. Her small breasts were hard, like pieces of ripe fruit. He rubbed his crotch, then approached the bed.

* * *

Lane Barrett met his seven men at the livery, before any of the others came along.

"We all know what we're gonna do?" he asked.

The men nodded their heads.

"Nobody's havin' any second thoughts, right?" he asked.

"Not for the amount of money we're dealin' with," one of them said. "No second thoughts."

The other men nodded their agreement.

"And anybody got a problem with what happens to Ben?" Lane asked.

There was some hesitation, then a man said, "Not as long as your plan works."

"It'll work," Lane assured them, "as long as we all act at the same time and according to plan."

"If somethin' does go wrong, he'll kill us," a third man said. "He's deadly with that gun."

"He'll be outnumbered eight-to-one," Lane reminded them. "He won't have a chance. Everybody just watch me, and don't lose your nerve."

Gordon Westin rode back to town after breakfast, accompanying Andrea Powell, who drove a buggy.

"Would you like me to get you a room at the hotel?" he asked.

"I can certainly register myself at the hotel," she replied frostily. He knew she was angry with her husband, but didn't know why he was receiving some of the overflow.

"I'll come by to check on you before I go back," he said.

"Fine."

He stopped at his office first to sit behind his desk and think while she went on to the hotel.

* * *

While Andrea Powell was registering at the hotel, a man came up next to her and said, "Excuse me."

She looked up at him. He was tall and brutish looking, and a shiver went through her as she looked into his steel gray eyes. The clerk looked on nervously.

"Yes?" she asked. "Can I help you?"

"I hope so," he said. "I told this feller to let me know if anyone connected with the Powell place came in here."

"And he just gave you the signal?" she asked, looking at the clerk, who looked away.

"Yeah."

"I happen to be Mrs. Powell," she said. "What can I do for you?"

"My name's Harcourt Smith," the man said. "I came here to meet a friend of mine named Joe Bags. When I got here, the law told me he's dead, and that he was workin' for your husband."

"That's true, I suppose," she said.

"You suppose? You don't know?"

"You'd have to talk to my husband," she said with a sigh, "or to his lawyer. His name is Gordon Westin and he's in his office now."

"Thank you, ma'am," Smith said. "If I can ask ya one more thing . . . where is his office?"

Westin was sitting with his feet up, wondering why Andrea was so cold to him, when the door opened and a man walked in. He was tall, hulking, and wore his gun like he knew how to use it. Westin let his feet drop.

"You Westin, the lawyer?" the man asked.

"That's right."

"Powell's lawyer?"

"Yes. What can I do for you?"

"Name's Smith, Harcourt Smith."

The man paused, as if the name should mean something to him.

"I don't know—"

"I'm a friend of Joe Bags," Smith said. "He sent me a telegram to come and help him. Seems I'm a little late."

"Yes," Westin said. "He's dead, along with four others."

"You know who killed him?"

"I know he was killed by Ben Randolph and his men," Westin said. "I don't know who actually pulled the trigger."

"According to the law hereabouts, nobody's doin' nothin' about it."

"Not entirely true," Westin said.

"Somebody is, then?"

"Yes," Westin said. "there is somebody, and I think he might be needing some help."

"And who would we be talkin' about?" Smith asked.

"Mr. Smith," Westin said, standing up, "why don't I buy you a drink?"

TWENTY-SEVEN

Clint Adams was sitting in one of a set of wooden armchairs on the front porch of Andrew Powell's house. The front door opened and Chelsea came out carrying a tray with a pitcher of iced tea and a couple of glasses.

"I thought you'd like something to drink," she said, putting the tray down on a small table at his elbow.

"Are you joining me?" he asked, noticing the second glass.

"No," she said, "but I expect Mr. Powell will be out here soon." She straightened up and looked out at the horizon. "Any sign of anyone?"

"Nothing."

"What are you looking for?"

"Well, given how many men he has, I'm looking for a cloud of dust."

"What if he comes alone?"

"That'd be preferred," Clint said, "but not very likely."

"Well," she said, "I'll leave you to it. Can I bring you a sandwich for lunch? I assume you'll be out here all day."

"That'd be nice," he said, "whenever you get a chance."

"Sure."

She went back inside and Clint poured himself some iced tea from the frosty pitcher.

He was halfway through the first glass when Andrew Powell came out.

"Iced tea?" Clint asked.

"I'd rather have a cognac, but sure," Powell said. He pulled the second chair over and sat down. "No sign of anything yet?"

"No," Clint said. "Do you anticipate Randolph coming with his full complement of men?"

"He'll bring somebody, that's for sure," Powell said.

"So no chance he'll come alone?"

"Not a chance," Powell said. "Not if he's still the man I knew."

"Did he have money when you knew him?" Clint asked. "Is that why you went into business together?"

"He had some contacts I was interested in," Powell said. "But no money of his own."

"So when you made those contacts and you didn't need him anymore, you cut him loose. Am I right?"

"Actually, you are," Powell said, "and I give no apology for that. It was just business."

"But you can't get Randolph to see it that way, can you?"

"I'm afraid not."

"Are you thinking of using that gun under your arm?" Clint asked. He had noticed the bulge under the man's arm when he first came out.

"I didn't use it the first time Randolph came to me," he said. "And I certainly didn't try for it when he brought me the five dead men. I'm thinking it may be time for me to get actively involved. Besides, you'll probably need some help."

"Can you hit what you shoot at?"

"I can't hit targets," the man said. "I'm not a sharpshooter, but I can hit something the size of a man."

Clint nodded. He didn't bother asking Powell if he could shoot at a man who was shooting back at him.

"Well, if it comes to that," Clint said, "just keep your eyes on me. Don't go for that gun unless I pull mine. Understand?"

"I understand."

"Good."

The two men sat there, drinking their iced tea in silence.

Harcourt Smith reined his horse in, causing Gordon Westin to do the same.

"What is it?" the lawyer asked.

"That way," Smith said, pointing to their left—west. "See that cloud of dust?"

"I see it."

"Only thing makes a cloud like that is a lot of men," Smith said. "What's that way?"

"Just a nothing little town called Ariza."

"Nothin'?"

"There's nothing there but a saloon and some falling-down buildings."

"Just the kind of place to hole up if you don't wanna be found."

"You think Randolph was there?"

"And he's ridin' this way," Smith said.

"Heading . . . to town?"

"He got any business in Brigham that you know of?" Smith asked.

"No."

"You know someplace where he does have business?"

"We both do," Westin said.

"Then we better get movin' if we wanna beat them there," Smith said. "Lead the way, lawyer."

Clint stood up.

"What is it?" Powell asked.

"Two riders."

Powell stood up.

"Just two?"

Clint nodded.

"I don't see them."

Clint pointed.

"I still don't—oh, wait . . . I see them. Can you tell who they are?"

"One looks like your lawyer," Clint said, although he was going more by the horse than the rider.

"And the other one?"

Clint squinted,

"I can't tell . . . I don't think I know him," Clint said. He looked at Powell. "Could it be Randolph?"

"I doubt it," the man said. "Why would he be riding here with Gordon?"

"Maybe," Clint said, "your lawyer doesn't have a choice."

"What do we do?" Powell asked anxiously.

"We relax," Clint said, "until we know what we're dealing with. Let's just let them get closer."

"All right."

"Remember," Clint said, "don't touch that gun unless I touch mine."

"I understand."

TWENTY-EIGHT

"It's not him," Powell finally said as the men came closer. "It's not Randolph."

"Okay," Clint said, "then you can relax."

"I'm relaxed."

He may have been relaxed at that moment, but just seconds earlier he'd been as jumpy as a cat.

"Now the question is," Clint said, "who is he and why is Westin bringing him here?"

However, as the two riders got closer, Clint was suddenly able to identify the other man.

"Well, I'll be—" he said.

"What? You know him?"

"Yes, I do," Clint said. "His name's Harcourt Smith. He makes his living with his gun."

"Did you send for him?"

"I didn't," Clint said, "But Joe Bags did. He's just a little bit late."

"But it's good that he's here, right?"

"We'll have to see," Clint said.

* * *

"Big house," was all Smith said as they approached it.

"Yes, it is."

Smith was more interested in the two men on the porch.

"The older man is Mr. Powell," Westin said. "The other man is—"

"Clint Adams," Harcourt said, cutting him off.

"You know him?"

"I do."

"Does he know you?"

"He does."

"There's not going to be trouble, is there?" Westin asked.

"Not from me," Smith said.

Westin decided to keep quiet until they reached the house.

Clint didn't move as the two riders reached the house. Powell shuffled his feet, but that was all.

The two men stopped their horses right at the base of the steps.

"Clint," Smith said.

"Court."

"Bags call for you, too?" the man asked Clint.

"Not me. When I got here, he was already dead. Got killed."

Smith looked at Powell.

"Did he die workin' for you?"

"Yes," Powell answered.

Then he looked at Clint.

"You workin' for him now?"

"I am."

"Why?"

"I figure to get the man who killed Bags," Clint said. "Why not get paid while I'm doing it?"

Smith stared at him a few moments, then said, "Makes sense."

"You want in?" Clint asked.

"Who pays me, him or you?"

"Him."

"Then I do."

"We're waiting for a man named Ben Randolph to show up," Clint said. "I'll explain it to you."

"How many men?"

"About twenty-five."

"Well, you better talk fast, then," Smith said. "We're about half an hour in front of a dust cloud."

"Then you better take care of those horses and come up here," Clint said. "I'll tell you over some iced tea."

"Iced tea?" Smith asked.

"I can do better," Powell said.

"Then let's get to it," Smith said, stepping down from his horse.

TWENTY-NINE

They sat on the porch drinking iced tea laced with whiskey while Clint told Smith what he knew. Powell and Westin sat off to one side, with the older man contributing here and there.

"So what you're tellin' me," Court said when Clint was done, "is that it's the four of us against maybe twenty-five men, and these two can't shoot worth a damn."

"That's what I'm telling you."

Smith looked at Powell.

"You better be payin' a whole lot of money."

"I am," Powell said.

"They're coming," Clint said, looking out at the approaching cloud of dust.

Smith had a look, too.

"Ten minutes, by my reckoning," he said. "Clint, you think we can come up with a plan in ten minutes?"

"I've got a plan."

"What is it?" Powell asked.

Clint didn't answer Powell. He looked at Harcourt Smith when he said, "Why don't we just kill them all when they get here?"

Smith stared back at him, then said, "Sounds like a plan."

When Ben Randolph came within sight of the house, he stopped his gang's forward progress. He could see four men standing on the porch.

"Looks like he got hisself some help," Lane Barrett said.

"One man is Powell, another is the lawyer," Randolph said. "That means he got maybe two guns."

"We can ride in and kill them right off," Lane said.

Randolph looked at Lane.

"You and your bunch ride with me," he said. "Tell the rest of 'em to stay here."

"Why go in shorthanded, Ben?" Lane asked.

"Never mind," Randolph said. "Eight of us will be plenty. We were plenty against the other five, weren't we?"

"That's a fact."

"Then we'll be able to handle these two, whoever they are."

"If you say so. I'll pass the word."

"You do that."

"They ain't all comin' in," Court said. "At least that's good."

"He's probably bringing his best guns," Clint said. "They'll do all the work. The rest are for show."

"You're probably right."

"Court, you got any problem with me taking the lead?" Clint asked.

"No," Smith said, "no problem. You got here first."

"Okay."

Smith looked at Powell.

"How good is Ben Randolph with a gun?"

"Very good," Powell said.

"Why would a businessman be good with a gun?" Clint asked.

"I never said Randolph was a businessman," Powell said. "I said I was in business with him."

"For his contacts," Clint said.

"Correct."

"So he's more gunman than businessman," Smith said.

"That begs the question," Clint said to Powell, "why would you cross a man like that in the first place?"

"It was business," Powell said, "just . . . business."

"Is there anything you wouldn't do in the name of business?" Clint asked.

"No," Gordon Westin said.

Ben Randolph, leading seven men, rode up to the house and reined his horse in. The twelve men eyed each other silently.

"Well, Andrew," Randolph finally said, "looks like you got yourself some more men. They must be pretty good, though. You only brought two this time."

"I brought as many as I thought I'd need," Powell said.

"Does this mean you've agreed to pay, Andrew?" Randolph asked.

"No," Powell said, "no, Ben, I'm not going to pay."

"Having five dead men laid at your feet didn't convince you?" Randolph asked. "Did you tell your two new men what happened?"

"We know," Clint said. "He told us."

Randolph looked at Clint.

"Are you the spokesman here?"

"You can talk to me."

"My name is Ben Randolph," the gang leader said. "These are my men. And further back are more of my men. How much is Andrew paying you to die?"

"I'd like to know which of your men killed a friend of mine named Joe Bags."

"Bags?" Randolph frowned.

"One of the five men you killed."

"Well," Randolph said, "that's really all I know. There were five of them, and they were killed. I don't know what their names were."

"But you gave the order," Harcourt Smith said.

"I suppose that's right," Randolph said. "What do you two propose to do about it?"

Smith looked at Clint.

"Who are you two anyway?" Randolph asked. "Maybe this time I should know your names before we kill you."

Clint nodded to Smith.

"My name's Harcourt Smith."

"Smith," Randolph said. "I've heard that name before."

He looked at Lane Barrett.

"Yeah, me, too," Lane said. "He makes his way with his gun."

"Like those other five?" Randolph asked.

"No," Lane said, "not like them at all."

The other men stirred, not sure where this was leading.

"And you?" Randolph asked, looking at Clint. "You somebody I should be concerned about?"

"My name's Clint Adams. I don't know if that means anything to you, or not."

The eight men remained silent, but exchanged glances. It seemed all of them wanted to speak.

"The Gunsmith?" Lane finally asked.

"That's right," Powell said, puffing out his chest. "The Gunsmith."

THIRTY

If Andrew Powell expected the men to turn and ride off at the sound of Clint's name, he was disappointed.

Clint didn't expect that either, but he saw the looks on the faces of the men Ben Randolph had with him. The leader himself was able to control his expression better.

"Impressive," he said finally. "The Gunsmith, and Court Smith."

He looked behind him for a moment, then back at them.

"I have seven men with me, and twice that waiting for me."

"Go ahead and call the others," Clint said. "You'll be dead by the time they reach us."

Randolph laughed.

"You think you can kill all eight of us before they get here?"

"I think we can kill most of you," Clint said, "starting with you."

"Who wants to be first?" Court Smith asked.

Before any of them could speak, or act, Randolph held up his hand.

"Take it easy, everyone," he said. "Nothing has to happen here. You may get me, Adams, but I'd get Andrew. Then who would pay you?"

"What do you want, Randolph?" Clint asked.

"You know what I want," he said. "At least, Andrew knows."

"That's not going to happen," Clint said.

"You're gonna stand in my way?"

"That's right."

"Just the two of you against twenty-five men?"

"Whether or not it's just the two of us remains to be seen," Clint said.

Randolph suddenly looked around, even up on the roof. His men followed, looking all around them.

"Guns on us?" Randolph asked.

Clint didn't answer.

"Look, do you know what he did to me?" Randolph asked.

"I've heard the story," Clint said.

"So what do *you* want?"

"I told you. I want the man who killed my friend, Joe Bags."

"So do I," Court said.

"So if I give you his killer, will that satisfy you both?" Randolph asked. "Would you then leave me and my old friend Andrew to conduct our own business?"

"You call showing up here with twenty-five men taking care of your own business?" Clint asked. "The answer to that question is no, I won't leave."

"I won't either," Smith said, although at that moment he wasn't sure why. Maybe he was just backing Clint's play.

"If you don't know which man was Joe Bags, that's okay," Clint said. "We'll take the killers of all five of them.

And then you can be on your way and forget your business with Powell."

"That ain't gonna happen," Randolph said. "I'll burn this whole house down first."

"You can try."

"You'd let me burn the house down with a woman inside?"

"You ain't burnin' nothin'," Smith said. "In fact, you better go back to your other men and tell them who they have to deal with here. They might change their mind about backin' you."

Randolph licked his lips, then compressed them. He looked at Powell.

"This ain't gonna work, Andrew."

"It's going to work better than the other five did," Powell said. "You aren't going to carry the bodies of these two men into my office, I guarantee that."

"I'll back that guarantee," Clint said.

"So will I," Smith said.

"Damn you all, then," Randolph said. "What happens next is on your heads."

Randolph wheeled his horse around and rode off, followed by his men.

"What do you think he meant by 'what happens next'?" Powell asked.

"He's just making threats," Clint said. "He needs to come up with a new plan now. That'll take time."

"So you don't think they'll come riding in on us now?" Powell asked.

"No," Clint said. "He's got to talk to his men. The seven he had with him heard our names. Now they have to tell the others." Clint looked at Smith. "Court?"

"I agree," Smith said.

"Then we can go into the house?" Powell asked.

"All but one of us," Clint said. "We'll need somebody on watch."

"But you said they wouldn't come today?" Powell said.

"But they'll come sometime," Clint said, "and we need to be ready."

THIRTY-ONE

Randolph gathered his men around him. He knew he had to tell them all the truth because Lane and his bunch knew it. They all listened intently while he told them what they were dealing with.

"The Gunsmith?" one of them said. "I didn't sign on to go up against him."

"He's only got one other man with him," Randolph pointed out.

"I heard of Court Smith," another man said. "He's damn good with a gun. I wouldn't wanna face both of those fellas at the same time."

"Well then, maybe you just came up with a plan," Randolph said.

"What plan?" Lane asked.

Randolph looked at Lane, and then back at the other men.

"We take them separately," Randolph said. "All we've got to do is separate them."

"And how do we do that?" Lane asked.

"Did you notice they weren't worried about us burning the house down with a woman in it?"

"So?"

"So, that means she ain't inside. She's somewhere else."

"Where?" Lane asked.

"Maybe Brigham," Randolph said. "We're gonna find her and use her to split them up."

"I still ain't keen on facing either of them," someone said.

"Any one of you," Randolph said, "who doesn't like twenty-five to one odds for the money I'm payin' you can light out right now."

He looked around at the assembled men, catching as many of them as he could right in the eyes.

"That's fine," he said, "but if you stay now, you stay for good, or you'll have me to deal with. I'll kill you before the Gunsmith has a chance to. You all got that?"

They muttered and nodded, and Lane said, "Yeah, we all got it, Ben."

"All right, then," Randolph said. "For now we head back to Ariza. I've got to plan this perfectly."

They all turned their horses and rode away from the Powell house.

"That's it," Clint said to the other three men on the porch. "They're heading out."

"You think they're quitting?" Powell asked.

"No," Smith said. "That Ben Randolph fella ain't gonna quit."

"I agree," Clint said. "They need a new plan, and they won't be back until they have one they think is perfect."

"Maybe that gives us a little more time," Smith said.

"Time?" Westin asked. "For what?"

"To get some more men," Clint said. "If Randolph comes at us with twenty or more men, we're going to need help."

"Can you get more men?" Powell asked.

"We'll have to see," Clint said. "There are probably some men in town who will hire out."

"But not gunmen," Westin said. "I mean, not as good with a gun as you two."

"No," Clint said, "but most of Randolph's men aren't gunmen either. We just need to offset the numbers he's going to throw at us."

"And how will you do that?" Powell asked.

Clint looked at him and said, "We'll start with your money. Also, you have some men working for you."

"Not ones who are good with a gun," Powell said.

"Right now we just need somebody to stand watch."

"I'll stay here until you find somebody," Smith said.

"Okay," Clint said, looking at Powell. "Let's go inside and talk about it."

Clint, Powell, and the lawyer went into the house.

THIRTY-TWO

Powell had three men working for him, mostly for maintenance around the house. He pulled the three of them in, told them what was going on, and what they wanted from them. Two of them said fine, they'd stay and stand watch. One of them didn't want any part of gunplay, and left.

With one of the men out on the porch on watch, and one in back of the house just in case, Smith was allowed to come back in.

They gathered in Powell's office and Clint said, "Your wife is in town, so she's safe if they set fire to the house, but Chelsea is still here."

"The cook?" Powell asked.

"That's right," Clint said. "Maybe she's just a cook to you, but she's a woman and doesn't need to be here when the lead starts flying."

"Yes, of course," Powell said. "Someone will have to take her to town."

"I'll do it," Westin said.

"You'll have to take a different route to town," Clint

said. "They might be waiting for you on the main road."

Westin looked nervous.

"I'll ride in with them," Clint said.

"You think that's wise?"

"Smith will be here with you," Clint said. "You do everything he says and you'll be all right. Besides, I think Randolph is going to need at least a day to come up with a new plan."

"What if he hires more men?" Powell asked. "What if he comes with forty?"

"He can come with a hundred if he wants," Clint said. "Gangs are like snakes. If you cut off the head, the body dies. If we kill him, there'll be no one to pay them, and they'll scatter."

"Then why not do that?" Powell asked. "Sneak up on him and kill him?"

"Well, first," Clint said. "I don't bushwhack people. Second, I still want to see if we can find out who actually killed the other five men."

Powell looked at Smith.

"I don't bushwhack people either," Court Smith said. "Every man I've ever killed has been facing me."

"All right," Powell said, defeated. "I'm paying you, so I have to go by what you say."

"I'll go and tell Chelsea to get packed to go to town," Clint said. "Is she in the kitchen?"

"She should be," Powell said.

Clint turned and left the room. As he did so, he heard Powell asking who was going to cook supper.

Chelsea was, indeed, in the kitchen, up to her elbows in flour.

"You better get cleaned up," Clint said as he entered.

TWO GUNS FOR VENGEANCE

"Why?" she asked. "Have you got something in mind?" She lowered her voice. "We could go in the cupboard."

"You're going to town," he said.

"Why?"

"So you'll be safe," Clint said. "There's going to be trouble here."

"Now?"

"Soon," he said. "Well, probably tomorrow. But I want you gone today."

"Am I riding to town alone?"

"No," he said, "I'll take you. You'll have to go upstairs and get packed now."

"And once you get me to town?"

"Then I'll come back here."

"Right away?"

"Well . . . we'll see," Clint said.

She walked up to him, took his face in her flour-covered hands, and kissed him.

"I'll be ready soon."

She left him standing there with white fingerprints on his face.

THIRTY-THREE

Clint went back to the office to wait for Chelsea with the other men.

"I'll ride back with you," Westin said.

"I want Gordon to check on my wife," Powell said.

"I could do that."

"I have some other work for him to do," Powell said. "Paperwork."

"Okay," Clint said. "Gordon, why don't you go out front and have that fellow get our horses while you spell him for the time being."

"Okay."

Clint looked at Smith.

"I'll be fine," Court said. "If Randolph shows up, I'll try my best to kill him."

"If he shows up?" Powell repeated. "But you said he wouldn't be back today."

"He won't," Clint said.

"Probably not," Smith said.

"What?" Powell said as the two men left the room. He

looked at Westin, who shrugged and followed Clint and Smith.

Rather than riding in a buggy into town, Chelsea chose to saddle a mare she said was hers. When she mounted up, she rode Western-style, and handled the horse well.

"Let's take the main road," Clint said to Westin.

"But you said—"

"I know what I said, but that was when you and Chelsea were going to ride in alone. With me along, I don't think anybody will try anything."

"Why not?" Chelsea asked.

"Randolph hasn't had time to form a new plan yet," Clint said. "Even if we do run into somebody, they'll probably just be on watch."

"Okay," Westin said. "It's your call."

Clint wasn't surprised that Randolph had not even put anyone on watch. With his plans in total disarray, it was no surprise he'd crawled back into his hole and taken all his men with him.

They rode into Brigham with no incidents. Clint took Chelsea to the hotel and got her a room. He told the clerk that Andrew Powell would be paying.

"Yes, sir."

He walked Chelsea to her room.

"Now don't go out unless you have to."

"Like to eat?" she asked.

"There's a café down the street. Use that."

"And where is Mrs. Powell?"

"She's also in this hotel."

"Can I go and see her?"

"If you like. In fact, it might not be a bad idea for you two to watch out for each other."

"You think those men might come for her? Or me?"

"Maybe her, not you. No offense."

"None taken."

Clint thought a moment, then said, "I'll have to get a man to watch over the two of you."

"Before you go back?"

"Yes."

"Then you'll be back to see me?"

"Yes," he said, "I'll be back before I leave."

"Good," she said, sitting on the bed, "I'll have something to look forward to."

"Don't worry," he said. "I don't think you'll be here very long. This whole thing is going to come to a head soon."

"And after that? You'll be leaving?"

"When it's all done, yes," he said. "It'll be time for me to go."

"Maybe me, too," she said. "Might be time for me to find a new job."

"You might be right," Clint said. "Sounds like things might change in the Powell household after this."

"They were headed that way long before this," she said.

"That's their problem," he said. "I just want to find out who killed my friend."

"Well," she said, touching his arm, "just be careful you don't get killed while you're doing it."

"That's always the first thing I remind myself when I get up in the morning," he told her. "Don't get killed. Remember what I said. Don't spend too much time outside the hotel."

"I'll remember," she said.

"I'll see you soon," he said, and left.

THIRTY-FOUR

Clint decided to go to the sheriff for protection for the two women.

"How are things goin' with you and Mr. Powell?" Sheriff Doby asked as Clint walked in.

"Just fine," Clint said.

"You solve that problem of his?"

"Not yet," Clint said, "but I could use some help."

"With what?"

"Mrs. Powell and her cook, Chelsea Piper, are across the street at the hotel. I'd like someone to keep an eye on them."

"It's my job to keep an eye on everybody in this town," the lawman said.

"Well, I need somebody to keep a special eye on them," Clint said. "Can you recommend anyone in town I could pay to do that?"

"Pay?"

"That's right."

"Well," Doby said, rubbing his jaw, "maybe I could take the time—"

"I'd rather have someone who doesn't also have to keep an eye on the town, thanks all the same. Just a suggestion would be good."

The sheriff hesitated, then said, "Maybe I have someone for you . . ."

Doby told Clint there was a small saloon at the north end of town, just an old door across some barrels used as a bar and a few tables.

As he entered, he saw it was even smaller than he'd been told. The bartender looked up at him without removing his elbow from the bar, or his chin from the hand. There were two men seated at a table, each with a beer in front of them.

"Help ya?"

"Beer any good?"

"It's cold," the barkeep said. "Best beer in town."

"I'll take one."

The first thing Clint noticed was that the glasses were clean. When he tasted the beer, it was, indeed, cold.

"Pretty good, huh?"

"Real good," Clint said. "I'm looking for a man named Dan O'Day—if that's a real name."

Clint had the feeling the sheriff may have been having a laugh at his expense.

"O'Day? Right there."

Clint turned, looked at the two seated men.

"Which one?"

"The back one."

The man in question was leaning over the table, staring into half a mug of beer.

"How long has he been sitting there?" Clint asked.

"Years," the bartender said. "Oh, do you mean—okay, he's been there a few hours."

"With that same beer?"

The barkeep nodded.

"Okay, give me another one, then."

"Comin' up."

Clint carried his beer and the extra one to the table. The man didn't move.

"Dan O'Day?"

There was a long moment and then the man slowly lifted his eyes from the mug. He was younger than Clint had expected, judging from the way he'd looked sitting at the table with his head bowed and shoulders hunched. He appeared to be about thirty-five.

"O'Day?" Clint asked, again. "Cold beer?"

The man looked at the mug and said, "For me?"

"Yup."

"Why?"

"I want to hire you."

"For what?"

"Can I sit?"

"Gimme the beer."

Clint handed it over and O'Day took a sip.

"Okay," he said, "sit. Whataya need?"

"I need a man to stand guard over a couple of ladies," Clint said. "The sheriff suggested you."

"The beer's mine no matter what?" O'Day asked.

"That's right."

"Okay, well," he said, pausing to sip again, "I think the sheriff is playing a joke on you."

"Why? Why would you think that?"

"Well, for one thing, he don't like me," O'Day said. "And if he suggested me to you for a job, he probably don't like you either."

"What's he got against you?"

O'Day hesitated, then said, "I used to be his deputy."

"What happened?"

"I quit."

"Why?"

"Because he's a bad lawman, and I told him so."

"But if you were a deputy, it means you know how to use a gun."

"That's the problem," O'Day said. "I used to be good with a gun, but since I quit, I've had a beer in my hand more often than a gun."

Clint studied the man for a few moments. He didn't really have time to start looking for somebody else.

"Hold out your hand," he said.

"What?"

"Your gun hand. Hold it out."

O'Day extended his right hand, palm down.

"That's pretty steady."

"That's because I've been drinkin'," O'Day said. "Once I dry out, my hand starts to shake."

"Okay, so don't dry out."

"What?"

"Look," Clint said, "I'll pay you good money to do this job."

"For how long?"

"Maybe a few days."

"And you don't want me to dry out?"

"Not completely," Clint said. "Not if it keeps your hand steady."

"What are you payin'?"

Clint told him.

"Well . . . what's the job?"

"I'll do it," O'Day said when Clint was finished, "although I don't know why the Gunsmith would trust a stranger with these two ladies."

"Remember, you have the sheriff's recommendation," Clint said.

"I explained that to you."

"Well," Clint said, "I think our arrangement will work for us and be a thumb in the sheriff's eye."

"That suits me," O'Day said.

"Finish your drink and I'll introduce you to the two women."

"I don't think I need to meet them," O'Day said, "but you can point them out to me. Do you know where they are now?"

"You want to start now?"

"Might as well."

"Let me give you some money—"

"No," O'Day said, "don't give me any money. I might just drink it away. You can pay me after."

Right then Clint thought he'd made the right decision.

THIRTY-FIVE

Clint and O'Day stopped outside the small café down the street from the hotel. Clint looked in the window and was surprised to see both Chelsea and Andrea sitting together at a table.

"Pretty ladies," O'Day said. "Which one is Mrs. Powell?"

"The one on the left," Clint said. "Do you know Powell?"

"Ran into him once or twice when I was wearin' a badge," O'Day said.

"Well," Clint said, "all you've got to do is keep them alive until I tell you the job's done."

O'Day looked at Clint with bloodshot eyes, but steady hands. Clint knew the sheriff was probably trying to stick him with a drunk, but he doubted that the lawman would steer him toward someone who might be bought off by Ben Randolph.

"You can depend on me, Clint," O'Day said.

Clint was usually a good judge of character, so he said, "I know I can, Dan."

"You might as well let them know I'll be watchin' them," he said, "but tell them not to look for me."

"Okay. Thanks, Dan."

"I guess I should thank you for gettin' me out of the saloon."

"Mr. Adams," Andrea Powell said as Clint approached their table.

"Join us, Clint," Chelsea said.

"Are you here to sound the all-clear?" Andrea asked.

"Not at all," he said, sitting between them. "Nothing has happened yet. I'm here to tell you that I have a man watching you both. He'll protect you."

Andrea looked around and asked, "Where? Who is he?"

"You don't need to know who he is," Clint said, "and if he's doing his job right, you'll never see him."

"Very mysterious," Andrea said.

"I just want to do what I can to keep you safe while I get back out to the house."

"We're very appreciative," Andrea said, "Is, uh, Gordon going back out with you?"

"That's up to him," Clint said. "I don't really know."

"When are you going back?" Chelsea asked.

"Right now."

"Be careful," she said.

"I will."

Andrea looked from Chelsea to Clint and back, and Clint knew that he was going to be the subject of a discussion when he walked out.

"If you need anything, go to the sheriff," Clint said.

"My husband says he is useless," Andrea pointed out.

"That may be, but he's still the sheriff," Clint said. "He's the one you go to when you're in trouble."

"All right."

Clint stood and said, "Enjoy the rest of your meal, and I'll see you both soon."

He turned and left. Once outside, he peered in the window, saw the two women sitting with their heads together, speaking urgently.

He walked away and headed for the lawyer's office.

"I'm riding back to the house," Clint said as he entered the office. Westin was seated behind his desk, but didn't seem to be doing anything in particular. "Are you coming?"

"I don't know," Westin said.

"What's the problem?"

"I don't know how much help I'd be," the lawyer said. "I'm not very good with a gun."

"It might be enough help for us to just have another body," Clint said, "but I have an idea."

"What is it?"

"Why don't you stay in town and try to hire some help?"

"I—I don't know how to hire gunmen."

"All you need to do is hire men with guns," Clint said. "If we can provide a show of force, along with Court Smith's and my reputations, it might change the minds of some of Randolph's men."

"You want his men to desert him."

"Yes."

Westin sat forward in his chair, suddenly excited about possibly being of help.

"I can do that."

"Good."

"What do I pay them?"

"A hundred dollars each should do it," Clint said.

"That's cheap," Westin said.

Only compared to what Powell was paying Clint and Smith.

"I'm going back right now," Clint said. "When you have five or six men, send them out."

"Should I come with them?" Westin asked.

"Only if they need you to show them the way," Clint said.

"And how many do I try to get?"

"See if there are a dozen men in town who can use a hundred dollars," Clint said, "but don't hire a man named Dan O'Day."

"The deputy?"

"Ex-deputy. I've already got him watching the women to keep them safe."

"He used to be a good man," Westin said.

"I think he still is."

"I hope you're right. You think Randolph will send someone after Andrea? To use her as a hostage?"

"Maybe, but I doubt it. I think he'll come directly at us."

"I hope so," Westin said.

Clint headed for the door.

"You just start hiring men and send them out to the house."

Westin stood up and said, "I'll get right on it."

As he rode back out to the house, Clint wasn't at all sure they'd have time for extra men to arrive. However, it would probably take a man like Ben Randolph overnight to come up with a new plan. He was also going to have to make sure all his men were still dependable, especially after hearing Court Smith and the Gunsmith were involved. If things went right, maybe there'd be a mass desertion during the night. That would mean Randolph would need to hire more men, or make his move shorthanded.

Clint figured Randolph probably had six to eight men with him who could actually use a gun well. The rest were just filler, and those were the ones who would leave. If eight men came at them, it would be the best eight men in the bunch.

But eight would still be better than twenty or more.

THIRTY-SIX

When Clint got to the house, Smith was sitting out on the porch. Andrew Powell was nowhere to be seen.

"Where are the other two men?" Clint asked, reining in.

"One's in the back, I'm spellin' the other one. What's goin' on in town?"

"Not much." Clint told Smith how he'd hired someone to keep an eye on Andrea and Chelsea. He also told him what Gordon Westin would be doing.

"You think we can get some extra men out here in time?"

"I figure we've got overnight," Clint said. "Randolph should be back tomorrow."

"I hope so," Smith said. "I'd like to get this over with, and find out who killed Bags."

"So would I," Clint said. "I'm going to take care of my horse and then I'll spell you."

"Okay. Thanks."

"What's Powell doing?"

"Who knows? We didn't talk while you were gone. I think he's just waitin' for you to get back."

"I'll talk to him after I see to my horse, then I'll come out and spell you."

"No rush," Smith said. "I have nowhere else to go."

Clint found Powell in his office, sitting at his desk with a glass in his hand.

"Scotch," Powell said. "Good scotch. Care for some?"

"Why not?"

Powell held up the bottle. Clint went to the sidebar to fetch a glass, carried it to the desk. Powell poured two fingers of brown liquid into the glass.

"Thanks."

"How'd things go in town?" Powell asked.

Clint sat down and told him.

"You hired a stranger to guard my wife?"

"He's okay."

"How do you know?"

"I'm a good judge of character."

"I hope so."

"I also left it to your lawyer to hire us some more men."

"Gordon? He's not qualified to do that."

"He's qualified to hire men with guns. That's all we need."

Clint finished the scotch and set the glass down on the desk.

"More?" Powell asked.

"No, and I suggest you don't have any more either," Clint said, standing. "We don't know when Randolph is going to hit, and I need you to be sober."

"You said he wouldn't come until tomorrow."

"I also said he wouldn't send anyone to town to grab your wife," Clint said. "I'm guessing on both counts." Clint reached out and grabbed the bottle of the desk. "No more."

"Fine."

"And I think you should take a turn on watch," Clint said. "We need everyone."

"As you wish," Powell said, standing. He lost his balance for a moment, making Clint wonder how many drinks he'd had.

"I'm all right," Powell said, reading Clint's look.

"Then relieve your man in the back. Someone will relieve you in two hours."

"Fine."

Powell picked up his gun and walked out of the office.

Clint left the room, carrying the scotch bottle.

On the porch Clint said to Smith, "Here. It's his good scotch."

"Thanks."

Smith took the bottle, had a healthy swig.

"That is good scotch."

Clint took the bottle back and sipped.

"Where is he?"

"I sent him in the back to relieve the man there."

"Taylor," Smith said. "His name's Taylor."

"And the other one?"

"Styles."

"I'll remember."

They passed the bottle back and forth a few more times before the scotch was gone.

"Did you work out some kind of password with the lawyer?" Smith asked.

"Damn," Clint said. "I should have." Now there was a chance that some of the men Westin hired might ride out and get shot.

"We'll just have to be careful we don't kill our allies," Clint said.

"I'll try my best," Smith said.

THIRTY-SEVEN

Randolph sat in the saloon in Ariza, talking to Lane Barrett.

"The others aren't gonna be much help," Lane said. "They're afraid of the Gunsmith."

"Tell them we'll pay them more."

"How much more?"

"Does it matter?" Randolph asked. "We're not gonna pay them anyway, remember?"

"Right. What about sending someone out there to watch?"

"No point," Randolph said. "We know they're there and they know we're comin'."

"Yeah, but—"

"Look," Randolph said, "we're just gonna ride in there and take them. And I want the house burned to the ground."

"What if there's money in the house?"

"Most of his money is in the bank in Brigham," Randolph said, "and if we have to, we'll burn that to the ground, too."

* * *

Andrea and Chelsea had the desk clerk buy them a bottle of whiskey and bring it to Andrea's room.

"Are you worried about him?" Andrea asked, pouring the liquor into two glasses.

"Who?"

"Clint," Andrea said, handing Chelsea one of the glasses. "It's all right. I saw him go into your room."

"Well then . . . yes, I am," Chelsea said. "Are you worried?"

"About Andrew?" Andrea asked.

"Or . . . someone else."

"You know, don't you?"

"I'm sorry," Chelsea said. "I saw you . . . once."

"Then yes, I am worried. About all of them. That man Randolph has already killed five men. And we just have to . . . sit here and wait."

"Don't worry, ma'am," Chelsea said. "Clint can handle them."

"He's only one man, Chelsea," Andrea said. "And call me Andrea."

"I know he's one man, Andrea," Chelsea said, "but what a man."

THIRTY-EIGHT

The night passed without incident.

Dan O'Day stayed across the street from the hotel, occasionally crossed and used the alley to check the back. By morning he was certain nothing had happened to the women inside.

He was hungry. Even more, he was thirsty, but he was determined to satisfy Clint Adams's confidence in him. He didn't know how he had earned it, but he wanted to justify it.

Court Smith came out of the house and found Clint on the front porch. He was wearing his gun belt and carrying a rifle. Clint's rifle was cradled in his arms.

"How long have you been up?" he asked.

"Not long," Clint said. "I spelled Styles about an hour ago."

"I'll go inside and make some coffee, then."

"Sounds good."

"Strong?"

"The stronger the better."

Smith went inside. Fifteen minutes later Andrew Powell came out. He was wearing a shirt and jeans, and a gun belt. He was also carrying a rifle. It was the first time Clint had seen him in anything but a suit.

"Anything?" he asked.

"No sign."

"I smell coffee in the house."

"Court's making it. He'll bring it out."

"Where are Taylor and Styles? Shouldn't they be out here?"

"They needed some sleep," Clint said. "They'll be out soon."

"No men from town yet?"

"None."

"If word has gotten around—"

"I know," Clint said, cutting him off. "We won't get any help."

"Can we stand against them?"

"Maybe," Clint said.

"Maybe?"

"Depends on how many of them come," Clint said, "and how they come."

"Is there anything we can do but wait?"

Clint hesitated, then said, "Maybe. I've actually been thinking about that for the past hour."

"And?"

As the door opened and Court Smith came walking out, Clint said, "Still thinking."

They drank coffee on the porch, and when Taylor and Styles reappeared, Clint said, "I have an idea."

"What is it?" Powell asked.

"We stop waiting."

"And do what?"

"We go after them," Smith said.

"Right," Clint said.

"Just us?" Styles asked. "After all of them?"

"Not all of them," Clint said. "Some of Randolph's men will have left, or will be leaving today."

"Still . . ." Taylor said.

"And we'll have surprise on our side," Clint said. "They'll never expect us."

"All we have to do," Powell said, "is know where they are."

"Ariza," Smith said.

They all looked at him.

"Well, that's the direction they came from. Any other towns that way?"

"Not in Arizona," Powell said.

"They wouldn't go over the border to hide out," Clint said.

"They couldn't," Powell said. "Ariza's the only place they could hide out that would be less than a day's ride from here."

"Then that's where we'll find them," Clint said.

Powell asked, "But what about the house? What if they come here, and we miss them?"

"It's just a house," Clint said. "There won't be anyone here for them to threaten. Besides, we won't miss them."

"How do you know?" Powell asked.

"They make a considerable dust cloud when they travel," Smith said.

"We'll see it, as long as we're heading for Ariza," Clint said. He looked at Taylor and Styles. "Come on. Let's saddle some horses."

The two men looked at Powell.

"Look," Clint said, "if we're all going to come out of this alive, you're going to have to do what I say without looking at him first."

"He's right," Powell said. "You'll take your orders from Mr. Adams until this is all over."

"But you'll still be payin' us, right?" Styles asked.

"Yes," Powell said. "You'll both get a bonus."

Styles looked at Taylor and said, "Let's saddle some horses."

THIRTY-NINE

Gordon Westin sat behind his desk in abject misery. Word had gotten around that the Powell house was going to be attacked and burned, and everyone was going to be killed.

Because of that, he hadn't been able to hire one man.

He had failed.

Abruptly, he stood up and rushed from his office. He had to check and make sure that Andrea was all right.

Andrea and Chelsea had spent the night in their own rooms. In the morning they met in the lobby and went to breakfast together. They were sitting in the same café when the lawyer entered, a little wild-eyed until he saw them.

"Gordon," Andrea said. "Join us?"

He sat down with them.

"I'm glad you're all right," he said, then added, "Both of you."

"Thanks," Chelsea said.

"You don't look so good," Andrea said. She poured him some coffee.

"Clint gave me one job to do, and I failed."

"What was that?" Chelsea asked.

"Hire some more men, send them out to the house to help."

"And how many did you get?" Andrea asked.

"None."

"None?" Chelsea said.

"The word has got around that everyone at the house will be killed," he said. "Nobody wants to go, no matter how much I offered them."

"Then we have to go!" Chelsea said.

"She's right," Andrea said.

"What? What do you mean?"

"You, and us," Chelsea said. "Three more guns on their side."

"We can't—"

"If you won't go with us, we'll go without you," Andrea said.

"No, No," Westin said. "I'll go, but . . . just us?"

"Well," Chelsea said, "there is one more man."

O'Day followed the women to the café, then saw the man join them. He stood across the street until one of the women came outside and started waving. At him?

He crossed the street.

"Are you the man Clint hired to protect us?" Chelsea asked.

"That's right, ma'am," he said. "I'm Dan O'Day."

"Come inside and have some breakfast," she said. "We have to talk."

Over breakfast they told O'Day what they wanted to do.

"And you want me to go with you?" he asked.

"Four more guns," Chelsea said. "It has to be helpful."

"Well," O'Day said, chewing the last of his eggs, "if you decided to ride out there, I guess it would be my job to follow you."

"So you might as well ride along with us," Andrea said.

O'Day shrugged and said, "Okay."

Both women smiled.

"We better saddle up, then," Westin said.

O'Day looked at him.

"You're a lawyer, right?"

They walked to the livery, saddled their horses, and mounted up. Then they rode to the general store, where Andrea bought guns for her and Chelsea—pistols and rifles—and a rifle for O'Day. Westin had his own weapons.

Saddled up and armed, they left town and rode back toward the house.

Clint, Smith, Powell, Taylor, and Styles were mounted up and armed, gathered in front of the barn.

"What are we going to do when we get there?" Powell asked.

"We'll see what the situation is," Clint said. "Between here and there we'll see if we come across a place to stop them. If not, we'll have to stop them at the source. Ariza."

"But . . . how?" Powell asked.

Clint and Smith exchanged a glance.

"We'll figure that out along the way."

FORTY

Five riders were heading from the Powell house to the town of Ariza.

Four riders were heading from Brigham to the Powell house.

Ben Randolph was sitting in the saloon in Ariza, getting the bad news.

"What?" he said. "How many?"

"Eight."

"Eight men have left?"

Lane Barrett nodded.

"Must have ridden out during the night."

"So," Randolph said, "we still have seventeen. Plenty to do the job."

"There's been some talk . . ." Lane said.

"About what?"

"I don't think we're done losing men."

"What about your bunch?"

"Oh, we're still in."

"All right," Randolph said. "It'll save us the trouble of gettin' rid of the others later."

"So what do we do?"

"Get the remaining men saddled up and ready to ride," Randolph said. "Let's get this over with."

"Hold on," Smith said, lifting his arm.

"What is it?" Powell asked.

"Somebody's coming."

"Is it them?"

"No, it's not a large enough group," Clint said.

"Then who—"

"There!" Smith said, pointing.

"That looks like—" Powell started.

"It is," Clint said. "Your wife, your lawyer, and your cook."

"And another man," Smith said.

"That's O'Day," Clint said.

"The man you hired to watch the women?"

"That's right."

"Well," Smith said, "I guess this counts as watching them."

They waited for the others to reach them.

"What the hell are you doing?" Powell asked when the others reined in.

"I couldn't get any help," Westin said.

"Nobody?" Clint asked.

The lawyer shook his head.

"No one's willing to come out and help, not after the word got around."

"So you decided to bring them?" Powell asked.

"No, sir," Westin said. "They brought me."

"I insisted," Andrea said. "You need guns."

Clint looked at O'Day.

"You told me not to let them out of my sight."

Clint studied the man, decided he was sober.

"It's okay, Dan," he said.

"The two of you should go back to the house," Powell said. "Gordon, take them."

"And if Randolph hits the house while we're there?" Andrea asked. "We're safer with you."

"Where are you going?" Chelsea asked.

"We decided to attack instead of waiting," Powell said.

"Attack where?" Westin asked.

"Ariza," Clint said.

"Ah," Westin said, "that's where Smith and I saw them coming from. At least, from that direction."

"All right," Clint said, "we'll all go, but let's leave now before we miss them."

FORTY-ONE

Clint and Smith rode alongside each other, leading the rest.

"You know some of these people are going to end up dead," Smith said.

"Maybe."

Smith remained silent.

"Okay, probably," Clint said.

"We should leave them all and go in alone," Smith said. "Before they know we're around, we could take care of a bunch of them."

"That sounds like a good idea," Clint said, "but let's find a good place to leave them."

"Besides," Smith said, "I'm sure a bunch of them have left by now."

"Oh, yeah," Clint said. "The odds are probably better."

Yeah, he thought, more like fifteen to two rather than twenty-five to two. A lot better.

Clint said, "Here." He jumped off Eclipse and studied the trail.

"Yeah," Court agreed, looking around.

Everyone else reined in and turned.

"Okay," Clint said, "the rest of you are going to stay here."

"Here?" Powell asked. "Why?"

"Because we're going into town," Clint said. "If they get past us, you can bushwhack them here."

"Here," Andrea said.

"This road is well traveled," Clint said. "And recently, by a lot of horses. It must be them. So they'll come this way. Hide yourselves on either side of the road, and wait."

"And then what?" Chelsea asked, getting off her horse and flexing her feet.

"When they come by, open fire. Get as many of them as you can."

"Kill them?" she asked.

Everyone looked at her.

"That *is* what this is all about," Powell said.

"But . . . I'm a cook."

Clint walked over to her and put a hand on her shoulder.

"Don't worry," he said. "You won't have to."

They all watched as Clint remounted Eclipse, and rode off toward Ariza with Court Smith.

About half an hour later Smith said, "There it is."

"Little town."

"Yeah."

"Looks like a bunch of men and horses on the street."

"Looks like."

Clint looked at Smith.

"You ready?"

Smith pulled out his rifle and said, "I'm ready. Right down Main Street?"

Clint nodded. "Right down Main Street."

* * *

Randolph counted. He had fifteen men left. Sixteen counting him. The dirty cowards.

As his men were mounting up, Lane Barrett came over to him and said, "Hey, boss. Look."

"What?"

Barrett pointed.

Coming down Main Street were two riders.

Just two.

FORTY-TWO

Clint and Court Smith rode down the street toward the men, some of whom were mounted, some still on their feet.

"They're crazy," Randolph said.

"It's Court Smith," one of the other men said, "and the Gunsmith."

"They're just ridin' in, like nothin's goin' on," another man said.

"Take it easy," Randolph called to his men. "They're just two men."

Three of the remaining men exchanged a look, and then started walking away, slowly at first, and then they broke into a run.

"Damn it," Randolph said, drawing his gun.

"What are you doin'?" Lane asked.

"I'll kill the next man who tries to run," he yelled out.

All the men turned and looked at him, then down the street at the two riders.

"You face them, you might die," Randolph said, "but I'll kill you for sure."

"You're one man," somebody said.

Lane Barrett pulled his gun, and then the men who followed him did the same. Suddenly, more than half the men had guns in their hands.

"The rest of you skin those hoglegs or die," Randolph said.

Slowly, they all drew their weapons. Randolph had twelve men.

"Why'd they come here?" Lane asked.

"What's the difference?" Randolph said. "We kill them, then we go for the house, and the bank. We go for it all."

"Yeah, okay."

There were four men left whom Barrett was planning to get rid of anyway.

"Let's send them down the street first," he suggested.

"Fine," Randolph said.

Lane walked over to them.

"You four, start walking."

"But—" one of them said.

Lane Barrett cocked the hammer on his gun, and the others followed.

"Move!" he said.

Clint and Smith watched as four men advanced on them. Behind them, another eight stood ready, along with Ben Randolph.

"Sacrifices," Smith said.

"Yes," Clint said. "Let's give them a chance to walk away."

"I think they'll take it," Smith said. "Look at the small steps they're takin'."

When they came within earshot, Clint said, "You men have a choice. Walk away or die."

One of them said, "Randolph will kill us anyway."

"He's puttin' you out here as a sacrifice," Smith said. "He's hopin' you'll get one of us while we get all of you."

"Walk away," Clint said. "We'll cover your back. Just drop your guns and keep walking."

The four men exchanged glances, then dropped their guns in the dirt and continued walking past Clint and Smith.

"Okay," Smith said, "the odds look a lot better now."

"Four to one," Clint said. "We've got them right where we want them."

They rode on.

"Those cowards!" Ben Randolph said.

"It's up to us, then," Lane Barrett said. "Spread out!"

Randolph watched as the eight men put some space between them. They fanned out across the street.

"Let me talk to them," Randolph said. "Maybe I can get them to throw in with us."

"We don't need them."

"If it comes to gunplay, they'll get some of us," Randolph said. "We already have less men to split with. We don't need to lose more."

"If we kill them," Barrett said, "we all get as big a rep. You ain't scared, are ya, Randolph?"

"*Scared* isn't the word," Randolph said. "I'm being careful."

"Sure sounds scared to me," Barrett said, "but go ahead, talk."

Ben Randolph moved forward to meet the two oncoming men.

FORTY-THREE

Clint and Court Smith reined their horses in as Randolph got closer.

"Looks like you've lost a good part of your forces, Randolph," Clint said.

"I've still got enough to do the job," Randolph said. "You boys ought to think about throwing in with us."

"Why would we do that?" Smith asked.

"The odds are against you," Randolph said, "and there's plenty of money to go around."

"You mean the money you think Andrew Powell owes you?" Clint asked.

"The money he cheated me out of."

"And you're planning on sharing that money with all your men?"

"They'll be getting paid," Randolph said. "I can pay you fellas, too."

"We're not doing this for money, Randolph," Clint replied.

"You telling me Powell's not payin' you?"

"Oh, he's paying us," Clint said, "but we're doing this to find out who killed our friend, Joe Bags."

"Well, hell," Randolph said, "I can tell you that. It was Lane Barrett gunned your friend down. Did it without warning, too."

"You didn't order it?"

"Look," Randolph said, "the reason I put together a force as large as this one was to try and avoid gunplay."

"You thought a show of force would do it for you?" Smith asked.

"I hoped it would. But Barrett, he jumped the gun, and his boys followed."

"His boys?"

"I hired them all together," Randolph said. "They're the bunch standing behind me. The rest of 'em weren't gunhands, which is why you scared them off. These men are gunmen, and they gunned down those five fellas, including your friend."

"And you just watched?"

"I can handle a gun," Randolph said, "but I was hopin' not to have to. But Powell's giving me no choice, especially sending you fellas in here."

"Well," Clint said, "it's still your play, Randolph. Call these men off and we can all walk away without a scratch."

"You'd let Barrett walk? And his bunch?"

"No," Clint said, "we'll take them in and let the law handle them."

Randolph shook his head.

"They wouldn't go for that, even if I would," he said. "I still want my money."

"If you think Powell cheated you in business, then take him to court," Clint said.

"Or draw your gun now," Smith said. "The choice is yours."

"I wouldn't draw on either one of you, let alone the two of you together."

"Then get your men to back down," Clint said.

"Don't think I can, but I'll try."

He backed off, turned his back, and approached his own men. Clint and Smith waited while he briefly spoke to a man they assumed was Lane Barrett, the man Randolph claimed had killed Joe Bags.

After speaking briefly, Randolph simply turned and spread his arms.

"Get ready," Smith said.

Clint just nodded then, assuming Smith was watching the men and not him, and said, "I'm ready."

"Looks like it's gunplay, boys," Randolph said. "Couldn't talk them out of it."

"You with us?" Lane Barrett asked.

"I'm paying the freight," Randolph said. "If you kill them, but I catch a bullet, there'll be nobody to pay you."

"Don't matter," Lane said. "Keep spread out!" he told his men, and they started forward.

"Here they come," Clint said. "A nice even number. I'll take the four on the left, you take the four on the right."

They watched as the men started toward them.

"That means I get Barrett," Smith said. "The one who killed Bags."

"Whatever," Clint said. "If that's the way it falls. I just want him to get what's coming to him."

"Don't worry about that," Harcourt Smith said. "He will."

FORTY-FOUR

The eight men advanced on Clint and Smith and then stopped.

"We'll give you men the same chance we gave those other four," Smith said. "Drop your guns and keep walkin'."

"Ain't gonna happen," Lane Barrett said.

Clint looked at him.

"You must be Barrett."

"Yeah, I'm Barrett."

"You killed a man named Joe Bags."

"So?"

"You admit it?"

"He was working for Powell, I was working for Randolph," Barrett said. "It was my job. Me and my men. We took care of the five men Powell sent after Randolph."

"But it was you," Smith said, "who killed Joe Bags, right?"

"Yeah, so what?"

"He was a friend of ours," Smith said.

Barrett looked at him, then at Clint.

"Both of you?"

"That's right," Clint said. "That's the only reason we're here."

"You other men hear that?" Smith asked. He pointed at Barrett. "This is the only man we're interested in. How many of you want to die for him?"

"Don't listen to him," Barrett called out. "We're in this together."

Clint and Smith remained silent, but watched the faces of the men. The problem with a large group of men—whether it was a gang, or a lynch mob—was that nobody wanted to be the first to die. That was the only reason a lawman with a shotgun could hold off a lynch mob by himself.

So when Smith asked, "Who wants to be first?" nobody stepped up.

"Guess that means you, Barrett," Smith said.

"Against you and him?"

"No," Smith said, "just me." Smith dismounted. "You and me."

Clint decided things had gone too far, so he didn't bother arguing the point. Besides, if Barrett outdrew Smith, it would fall to him anyway.

And he now had to watch the other seven men, plus Randolph.

The other seven were shifting their feet, wondering what to do.

"Why don't we just watch?" Clint said to them. "This should be interesting."

Smith stepped away from his horse and faced Barrett.

"You think I'm scared to face you one at a time?" Barrett asked. "I ain't scared."

"That's good," Smith said.

"'Cause after I kill you, I'll just kill him."

"If you manage to kill me, I don't care what you do after that."

Clint wasn't watching Smith and Barrett; he was watching the other men. So when Barrett went for his gun, Clint didn't see it. When there was one shot, though, he saw the other seven men flinch, and two of them went for their guns.

Clint drew and shot both men even before they were able to clear leather. The other five men flinched again. Three of them stepped back and raised their hands, and two of them actually put their hands up in front of them, as if to ward off bullets. Clint kept his gun on them, risked a look at Smith. He was standing over the fallen Lane Barrett, who was lying on the ground, blood pooling beneath him.

"Okay?" Clint asked.

Smith bent over the man, then straightened and said, "He's dead." Smith covered the other men with his gun.

"Okay," Clint said. "Drop your guns."

The five men took their guns from their holsters and dropped them in the dirt.

"Now go," Clint said.

"Where?" one of them asked.

"Anywhere! Just go!"

The five of them hurried away, three of them actually running.

Clint dismounted, Smith grabbed the reins of his horse, and they both walked over to Randolph.

"My turn?" Randolph asked. "Two against one?"

"You liked it when you had twenty men behind you," Clint said.

"Look, I never actually meant for there to be gunplay," he said.

"And you probably never intended to split all the money with your men either."

"Why should I?" Randolph asked. "It's my money."

Clint stepped forward and took Randolph's gun from him.

"I understand you're pretty good with this," Clint said.

"Not in your league," he said. "I never said I was."

Clint looked at Smith, who folded his arms and stared at Randolph.

"What do you think?" Clint asked.

"Kill 'im," Smith said.

"Wha—wait!"

"I'll kill him," Smith said, drawing his gun.

"Hey, no, you killed Barrett," Clint said, still holding Randolph's gun. "I get to kill this one."

"Hey, look," Randolph said, holding his hands out, "I'm just trying to get what's owed me."

"If you were in business with Powell," Clint said, "and you think he cheated you, then get it back the way a businessman would get it back. Sue him!"

Smith holstered his gun.

"You're not gonna kill me?"

"Not unless you try this again," Clint said.

"I—I didn't tell Barrett and his men to kill those men," Randolph said. "I mean, your friend. I just let Andrew think I did."

Clint had the feeling Randolph was one of those men who could hit a target, but didn't have the nerve to stand up against another man with a gun.

"Go to court, Randolph," he said. "Take Powell to court. To tell you the truth, I'd like to see you win."

Clint tucked Randolph's gun into his belt and mounted up.

"Hey, my gun!" the man said.
"You won't need it."
Smith mounted up, and they rode out.

Outside of town Smith said, "What are we gonna tell Powell?"

"To get ready to go to court," Clint said. "He doesn't have to worry about twenty men raiding his house anymore."

"What if Randolph doesn't go to court?"

"To tell you the truth, I don't really care," Clint said. "We got the man who killed Bags."

"But what if Powell doesn't pay you?"

"Did you do this for the money?"

"No."

"Neither did I," Clint said, "but I have a feeling he'll pay me. Don't you?"

Watch for

THE MAD SCIENTIST OF THE WEST

360th novel in the exciting GUNSMITH series
from Jove

Coming in December!